HOW TO
THINK LIKE
SHERLOCK

For Rosie – 'always the woman'

HOW TO
THINK LIKE
SHERLOCK

Daniel Smith

First published in Great Britain in 2012 by
Michael O'Mara Books Limited
9 Lion Yard
Tremadoc Road
London SW4 7NQ

A CIP catalogue record for this book is available from the British Library.

Papers used by Michael O'Mara Books Limited are natural, recyclable products made
from wood grown in sustainable forests. The manufacturing processes conform to the
environmental regulations of the country of origin.

ISBN: 978-1-84317-953-5 in print format
ISBN: 978-1-84317-971-9 in EPub format
ISBN: 978-1-84317-972-6 in Mobipocket format

3 4 5 6 7 8 9 10

Printed and bound by CPI Group (UK) Ltd, Croydon, CR0 4YY

Cover designed by www.lucystephens.co.uk
Illustrations by Aubrey Smith
Designed and typeset by Dave Crook

www.mombooks.com

CONTENTS

II: Building Your Knowledge Base

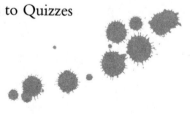

Introduction

Something strange has happened in the last few years. Sherlock Holmes – that uptight, cold, sexless sleuth who inhabited the grimy streets of London in the latter part of the nineteenth century and early part of the twentieth – has become cool.

Hollywood (in the form of Robert Downey Jnr) has got hold of Sherlock and made him tough, streetwise and even funny. Meanwhile, the BBC has given us Benedict Cumberbatch as a Holmes who oscillates between brooding moodiness one moment and manic energy the next. Cumberbatch's Holmes is the epitome of geek-sexiness.

For those of us who have loved the Holmes stories

since we first read them as children, and grew up enchanted by Jeremy Brett's spellbindingly faithful depiction of him on the screen, this has all come as something of a surprise. For years, the worship of Sherlock Holmes has been something undertaken by a significant but ultimately small community, often regarded with a mixture of curiosity and condescension by an unsympathetic world at large.

How did Sherlock Holmes win his newly-elevated status? There are doubtless many reasons, but surely one of the chief attractions is that he is just so remarkably smart. In a world where we are fed a diet of eye-wateringly dull reality television and are forced to bear witness to the tiresome antics of identikit celebrities, Holmes's fantastic feats of intellect and his complex and multi-layered psychology have never seemed more fascinating.

Holmes always knew he was a special case: 'No man lives or has ever lived who has brought the same amount of study and of natural talent to the detection of crime which I have done,' he famously declared. Those who witnessed his exploits at first-hand called him 'a wizard, a sorcerer!' and spoke of 'powers that are hardly human'.

But Holmes himself was reluctant to share his secrets, proclaiming: 'You know a conjurer gets no credit when once he has explained his trick and if I show you too much of my method of working, you will come to the conclusion that I am a very ordinary individual after all.' And even if he had shared, he had little faith in the ability of others to truly understand his methods: 'What do the public, the great unobservant public, who could hardly tell a weaver by his tooth or a compositor by his left thumb, care about the finer shades of analysis and deduction!'

But, of course, the public back then did not have access to a book such as this. In the pages that follow we will make a light-hearted but comprehensive exploration of the psyche, mental gymnastics and investigative techniques of the world's greatest consulting detective. Each section includes evidence from the original stories of Holmes's mental processes, along with all sorts of information, advice and tips on how you can more closely resemble him. A liberal spattering of quizzes and exercises should serve to keep you on your toes as you go along.

Nor need you be planning a life as a crimefighter to benefit from these pages. A great many of the skills that Holmes encapsulated are transferrable; we can all benefit from improving our mental dexterity, growing our memory capacity and learning how to interpret body language.

Read this book carefully and absorb its lessons. As Holmes himself declared: 'A man should keep his little brain attic stocked with all the furniture that he is likely to use, and the rest he can put away in the lumber-room of his library, where he can get it if he wants it.'

I:
Preparing the Mind

Understanding Sherlock

'I play the game for the game's own sake.'
'THE ADVENTURE OF THE BRUCE-PARTINGTON PLANS'

Dear old Sherlock has rather acquired a reputation over the years as an anti-social, unfeeling machine with a fearsome streak of arrogance. Such a description is not entirely unjustified. Even faithful Watson – in one of his more exasperated moments – described him as 'a brain without a heart, as deficient in human sympathy as he was pre-eminent in intelligence'. Then, in a more considered moment, Watson called him 'the best and wisest man whom I had ever known'.

In truth, Holmes nestled somewhere uncomfortably between these two descriptions. The ordinary, everyday world largely bored him, which could make him seem distant, disinterested and even callous. This was an unfortunate side effect of his on-going quest for excitement, for the unusual, for the sort of problem that could only be solved by his particular type of mind.

'I know, my dear Watson,' said Holmes in 'The Red-Headed League', 'that you share my love of all that is bizarre and outside the conventions and humdrum routine of everyday life.' It was this desire to rise above the mundane that so often drove him, sometimes onwards and upwards, sometimes into extreme danger and sometimes toward the terrible black dogs of his depression.

What cannot be in doubt is that the Great Detective took on all his work wholeheartedly, risking his own wellbeing in pursuit of his chief goal: defeating the worst criminal minds in the land. It was work that imperilled his life but which fulfilled a deep-seated need within him for intellectual challenge and heart-stopping adrenalin rushes. Take this short extract from 'The Boscombe Valley Mystery', which exquisitely captures Holmes as the thrill of the chase takes him over:

Sherlock Holmes was transformed when he was hot upon such a scent as this. Men who had only known the quiet thinker and logician of Baker Street would have failed to recognise him. His face flushed and darkened. His brows were drawn into two hard black lines, while his eyes shone out from beneath them with a steely glitter. His face was bent downward, his shoulders bowed, his lips compressed, and the veins stood out like whipcord in his long, sinewy neck. His nostrils seemed to dilate with a purely animal lust for the chase, and his mind was so absolutely concentrated upon the matter before him that a question or remark fell unheeded upon his ears, or, at the most, only provoked a quick, impatient snarl in reply.

There were many counterpoints to these moments of exhilaration. In the absence of suitable cases to invigorate his soul, Holmes displayed classic signs of depression and resorted to such unsavoury outlets for his energies as cocaine abuse. 'I get in the dumps at times,' he told Watson in *A Study in Scarlet*, 'and don't open my mouth for days on end. You must not think I am sulky when I do that. Just let me alone, and I'll soon be right.'

Equally destructive was his inability to consider his own basic physiological requirements when faced with an unresolved conundrum. In these circumstances, Watson memorably recorded how he 'would go for days, and even for a week, without rest, turning it over, rearranging his facts, looking at it from every point of view until he had either fathomed it or convinced himself that his data were insufficient'. Had he been a fan of those signs one sometimes finds in a certain kind of office environment, he might well have had one on his desk at 221B Baker Street that read: 'You don't have to be mad to work here. But it helps!'

All of which is to say, being Holmes was no easy

option, and to follow in his intellectual footsteps is not a journey for the faint-hearted. Holmes went about his work because he had no other choice – it was what made him who he was. Without it, there was little to define him. He alluded to his enormous sense of duty in *A Study in Scarlet*: 'There's the scarlet thread of murder running through the colourless skein of life, and our duty is to unravel it, and isolate it, and expose every inch of it.' Meanwhile, Watson would say of him that 'like all great artists' he 'lived for his art's sake'.

Do You Have the Personality?

'The strong, masterful personality of Holmes
dominated the tragic scene ...'
'THE ADVENTURE OF THE SOLITARY SCIENTIST'

We all make sweeping judgements about people. Him
over there is arrogant, her in the corner is needy, and as
for her friend ... well, where do I start?

The truth is that many of the judgements we make
about personality are instinctive and say as much about
us as they do about the person we are judging. The
study of personality can never amount to an exact
science. However, there is a body of long-established
research into personality that gives us a good basis for
discussion. So how does your personality type match up
against that of Holmes?

The founding father of the psychological
classification of personality types is Carl Jung, who
published his landmark study *Psychological Types* in 1921.
He outlined two pairs of cognitive functions. On the
one hand, the 'perceiving' (or 'irrational') functions of

sensation and intuition, while on the other hand, the 'judging' (or 'rational') functions of thinking and feeling. In layman's terms, sensation is perception as derived from the senses; thinking is the process of intellectual and logical cognition. Intuition is perception as derived from the subconscious while feeling is the result of subjective and empathetic estimation.

As if all this weren't quite complicated enough, Jung threw in another element: an individual's personality may be classified as extrovert (literally 'outward-turning') or introvert ('inward-looking'). In Jung's analysis, each individual has elements of all four functions to a greater or lesser degree, with each manifesting in an introverted or extroverted way.

Jung's philosophy was subsequently developed by many different parties over the years. Among them were the mother-and-daughter team of Katharine Cook Briggs and Isabel Briggs Myers, who developed the Myers-Briggs Type Indicator (MBTI), a trademarked assessment first published in 1962 that categorises personality into one of sixteen types based on four dichotomies:

Extraversion (E) – Introversion (I)
Sensing (S) – Intuition (N)
Thinking (T) – Feeling (F)
Judging (J) – Perception (P)

Personality types are represented by a four-letter code comprising the relevant abbreviations noted above. Of course, Sherlock Holmes never underwent such a personality test because he pre-dates them, is fictional, and would have had no truck with psychobabble. However, others have retrospectively attempted to assess him, with a broad consensus that he would probably lie somewhere between an INTP and ISTP classification: introverted, favouring intellectual reasoning over reliance on his feelings, and generally acting in response to information gathered rather than pre-judging a situation. The question of whether he best fits the sensing or intuition classification is much less clear. Incidentally, it has been suggested that Watson's profile best fits an ISFJ classification.

But what about you? Are you more of a Holmes or a Watson? Surely not a Moriarty? The MBTI test can be undertaken under the supervision of registered practitioners but there are many other Jungian-based tests that are free on the internet and can be self-administered. However, it is worth noting that personality testing should not be treated as a game nor as an exact science. Answering half a dozen questions on the internet cannot define your personality, for better or worse! But using a reputable personality test might offer you some useful insights into how you operate.

Developing an Agile Mind

'I am a brain, Watson. The rest of me is a
mere appendix.'
'THE ADVENTURE OF THE MAZARIN STONE'

While Holmes's personality and motivations are endlessly interesting enigmas, were it not for his remarkable intellectual capacity, you would not be here reading about him. There are plenty of interesting characters in life and literature, but very few able to solve an apparently unsolvable riddle like the Great Detective.

Alas, few of us can ever hope to match Holmes in the bulging brains department. That need not be a source of shame, though, for has there ever been a more penetrating intellect in literature than Holmes? 'You have brought detection as near an exact science as it ever will be brought in this world,' Watson told him in *A Study in Scarlet* (a piece of flattery that had even Holmes 'flushed up with pleasure'). 'Detection is, or ought to be, an exact science and should be treated in the same cold and unemotional manner,' Holmes himself would declare in *The Sign of Four*.

However, do not be fooled into thinking that Holmes is only concerned with cold analysis and the weighing up of empirical evidence. Holmes talked about his work as much in terms of art as science. It was a sentiment he returned to in 'The Problem of Thor Bridge', when he spoke of 'that mixture of imagination and reality which is the basis of my art.' In *The Valley of Fear*, he reiterated the necessity for creative thinking: 'How often is imagination the mother of truth?'

The great news is that if you don't feel like you are using your grey matter to Holmesian levels, you can train it to work better for you. This is not some self-help claptrap but scientifically proven fact. The brain is incredibly durable and can grow and change to cope with any number of new demands made upon it. You just have to make sure you get it into shape to meet new challenges.

Do you want proof? How about London's registered taxi cab drivers. To join the profession, applicants must undertake years of study known as 'the Knowledge', learning some 320 key routes encompassing thousands of streets within a six mile radius of Charing Cross in central London. Research students of 'the Knowledge' have typically shown an increase in the volume of the hippocampus (a part of the brain integral to memory).

The most famous winner of the television quiz was the 1980 champion Fred Housego, a cabbie who kept up his licence even after becoming a media celebrity. No wonder Holmes was accustomed to seeking out hansom cab drivers as fonts of information in so many of his cases!

Warming-Up

Regularly exercising your brain by playing mental games and doing quizzes has been shown to offer a defence against dementia in older people. But you are never too young to get into the habit. Here is a mixture of word and number games.

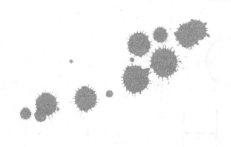

Quiz 1 – Letter Scramble

Can you rearrange the letters to spell four Holmes-related words? Each letter should be used exactly once in the resulting set. There are two words to find on this page and two on page 28.

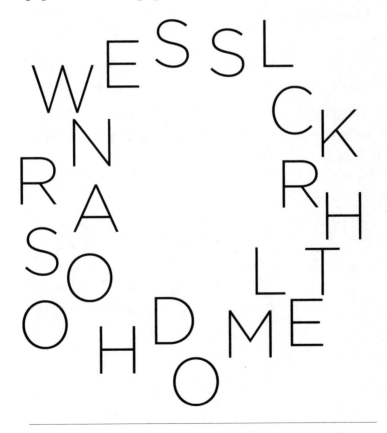

D A
N L A S G D
N A Y O
N Y I
G N L
S R S
M C G
T I A F

Quiz 2 – Number Sequences

Have a look at the following sequences of numbers.
Complete the sequence in each case.

1. 1, 2, 4, 8, 16, 32, _64_

2. 3, 9, 27, 81, 243, _486_

3. 1, 4, 9, 16, 25, 36, ___

4. 2, 3, 5, 7, 11, 13, _15_

5. 12, 33, 14, 30, 16, 27, 18, 24, 20, 21,___

6. 1, 2, 3, 5, 8, 13, 21, 34, 55, ___

7. 42339, 648, 192, 18, ___

Quiz 3 – Word Ladders

Here are a couple of word ladders. Starting with the word at the top of each ladder, can you change a single letter at a time to create a new word on each rung and arrive at the word at the foot of the ladder?

i) Cat

    ———

    ———

    ———

    ———

    Kid

ii) Game

    ———

    ———

    ———

    ———

    ———

    Foot

Quiz 4 – Word Wheel

To finish off your initial mental stretches, here is a word wheel. Copy it quickly onto a separate piece of paper. Each answer begins at the outside of the wheel and ends with the 'T' at the centre. When you have finished, the letters around the edge of the wheel should spell a familiar name.

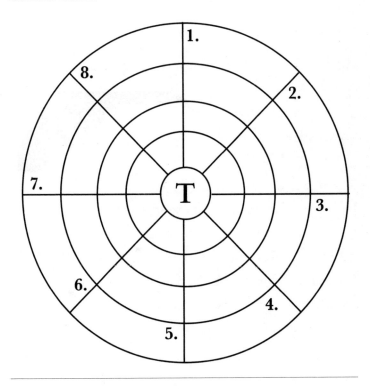

1. A first version.
2. Sunday lunch?
3. A popular card game.
4. Head of a monastery.
5. A characteristic.
6. Animal once prized for its fur.
7. Not discreet.
8. As dark as ...

Being Alert to the World Around You

'You see, but you do not observe. The distinction is clear.'

'A SCANDAL IN BOHEMIA'

Holmes's powers of observation were unmatched. He could scan a scene and alight on a telling detail that countless others had missed. He stated as much in 'The Boscombe Valley Mystery': 'You know my method. It is founded upon the observation of trifles.'

Some of us are born more observant than others but

it is nonetheless an ability that can be developed by hard work and dedication. Seeing – that is, perceiving with the eyes – is easy; observation – absorbing into your brain the data provided by your eyes – is much more taxing. Could you say what your nearest-and-dearest was wearing the last time you saw them, or what the colour of the last car that passed you was? What is the registration number of your next-door neighbour's car? As Holmes remarked in *The Hound of the Baskervilles*, 'The world is full of obvious things which nobody by any chance ever observes.'

If it is not a skill that comes easily to you, try consciously 'observing' in your daily life. If you're on a bus or sitting in a café, look at those around you (while trying not to appear like a crazed, staring stalker!). The more you practise the skill, the more natural it will become. Holmes was the undisputed master of this particular talent. Consider 'The Adventure of the Second Stain', in which our intrepid hero spots the lack of correlation between a bloodstain on a carpet and the floorboards beneath. It was this spot, missed by a troop of investigating policemen, that paved the way to the case's ultimate conclusion. Similarly, in 'The Disappearance of Lady Frances Carfax', Holmes makes a crucial observation about the depth of a coffin, though in the process rues the fact that he had not made his observation earlier: 'It had all been so clear, if only my own sight had not been dimmed.'

Keeping an Ear to the Ground

'My night was haunted by the thought that somewhere a clue, a strange sentence, a curious observation, had come under my notice and had been too easily dismissed.'

'THE DISAPPEARANCE OF LADY FRANCES CARFAX'

Just as important as developing your visual observation skills is improving your listening abilities. After Holmes had made the observation above in the case of Lady Carfax, he revealed that 'in the gray of the morning, the words came back to me', recalling an apparently off-the-cuff utterance from the previous day that would serve to help him resolve the case. In another story, 'The Adventure of the Speckled Band', he understands the importance of a 'low, clear whistle' in the dead of night better than any other figure in the story, with the exception of the perpetrator of a terrible crime. In the same way that Holmes could attach meaning to what his eyes saw like few others, he could grasp the connotations of sound quite magnificently (even when that sound was relayed to him by a witness rather than heard by his own ears).

One of the most famous observations in the whole of the Holmes canon reminds us that when we listen, it may be something that we don't hear that proves just as important as something we do hear. The observation is that concerning 'the curious incident of the dog in the night-time', namely the dog that didn't bark in 'Silver Blaze'. For most of us, the silence of a dog would be suggestive of very little but when this detail was discerned by the Great Detective, he was able to read much into it:

I had grasped the significance of the silence of the dog, for one true inference invariably suggests others. The Simpson incident had shown me that a dog was kept in the stables, and yet, though someone had been in and had fetched out a horse, he had not barked enough to arouse the two lads in the loft. Obviously the midnight visitor was someone whom the dog knew well.

As with improving your visual observation, the key to listening better is to consciously practise. We listen in two ways: passively – when we listen to the radio, sit in a lecture or are walking down the street – and actively – for example, when we are participating in a dialogue.

There are a few simple exercises you can use to become a better listener. Tune in to the hourly news bulletin on the radio. Really focus in on what is being related. When the broadcast finishes, switch off the radio and jot down some notes about what was said. Can you remember each of the stories in the right order? And can you recall the broad subject or have you retained some serious detail from each? When you begin, you might be rather shocked by how little has soaked in. But if you keep up the practice for a while, you will likely see some striking improvement. Similarly, sit in your garden on a summer's afternoon.

Close your eyes but keep your ears open. Note all the different sounds that you can hear, whether man-made or from nature. Such an exercise can help you become better attuned to the environment around you.

Improving your listening skills when you are part of a dialogue is a different challenge altogether. For the majority of us, when we converse we are more interested in being heard than hearing. But by being this way, we risk missing out on learning lots of new information that might prove very valuable to us. Here are a few tips for improving your listening skills when in conversation:

Ask questions
That way, you encourage the other person to speak and yourself to listen.

Don't interrupt
Avoid the temptation to interrupt, even if it is to agree with the other person. Listening and speaking at the same time is a very difficult skill to master.

Focus on the speaker

It sounds so obvious but think how often you have been introduced to someone only to forget their name a moment later.

Cut out distractions

If you want to really listen to someone, try to engage in conversation in a place where there isn't a television showing the football over their shoulder, or where the latest object of your affections isn't visible. Keeping eye contact with the speaker is a good way of maintaining your listening.

Repeat it

Strange as it sounds, repeating something of particular interest that has been said can help lodge it in your mind. You can repeat it quietly to yourself so as not to unnerve the speaker by seeming to mimic what they are saying.

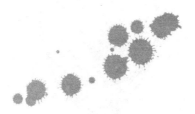

One of the great advantages of becoming a really good listener is that it builds bonds of trust with those you are listening to and will encourage them to listen to you in turn.

Quiz 5 – Not a Pretty Picture

In this exercise, take a minute to study the artist's impression of Dangerous Dave, a notorious robber. Reproduce Dave's face on page 41, or on a separate sheet of paper.

Reading Between the Lines

'I read nothing except the criminal news and the agony column.'
'THE ADVENTURE OF THE NOBLE BACHELOR'

It is probably fair to assume that Holmes made the above statement somewhat archly. Able to pluck just the right fact at the most opportune moment, he clearly had a significant breadth of reading. However, his quote about reading only news and gossip columns is suggestive of his ability to fix his focus on the material most useful to the job in hand. But rather than restricting his reading, it is far more likely that Holmes was an accomplished exponent of speed reading, able to digest large amounts of text at a high tempo and extract the information he required.

Studies suggest that an average adult reading speed is somewhere between 175 and 350 words per minute. The trick to speed reading is not merely to see more words in a shorter space of time, but to become more efficient at reading. It is all well and good to scan your eyes over, say, 500 words per minute, but not much use if the meaning of those words does not sink in at such a pace.

Here are a few ideas as to how to become a more efficient reader:

Read in an atmosphere conducive to concentration

Go somewhere quiet. Turn off the television, the radio, your telephone … anything that might distract you.

Learn to chunk!

When we learn to read, we do so in a word-by-word form. However, we are capable of reading blocks of words. Indeed, it has been argued that reading in blocks makes meaning clearer than focussing on each individual word. When an adult reads, their eyes tend to take in more than one word at a time, often scanning ahead of where they think they are in the text. Try it as you read now!

Relax

Typically, your gaze as you read will encompass about four or five words. Now hold this text further away from you and relax your gaze. You may well find you absorb still more words into each block. Your peripheral vision might even take in the end of a line while you are reading in the middle of it. With practise, you should be able to read in chunks of text, significantly cutting down the time required to scan a page.

Learn to focus on key words

Take the following line: 'This book contains lots of information about the famous detective Sherlock Holmes.' What are the most important words? Well 'book' tells us what we are talking about, while 'information' gives us a pretty good idea of the type of contents and 'Sherlock Holmes' gives us the specific subject. The other words, while all helpful in their ways, might justifiably be scanned over by a speed reader.

Stop sub-vocalizing

Many of us do something called 'sub-vocalization'. This means that a little voice in our heads says each word as we read it. A proficient reader really doesn't need to do this. Your brain understands a word quicker than you can say it. Here is an interesting experiment to show you why we needn't get caught in the minutiae of words as we read. Consider the following passage of apparent gobbledygook:

I'ts qtuie psolbiese to mkae ssnee of tihs scenetne eevn thguoh olny the fsrit and lsat ltreets of ecah wrod are werhe tehy slhuod be.

Some people are able to discern its meaning almost instantly, while to others it will seem like nothing more than gibberish. So how do some people manage to understand it? Many of us do not read every letter of a word as we scan text. In fact, often we only need the first and last letters of a word. Our brains then do their magic and, by feeding off a mixture of accumulated experience and immediate context, are able to predict what each word is likely to be. (For the record, the passage reads: 'It's quite possible to make sense of this sentence even though only the first and last letters of each word are where they should be.') Sub-vocalization is a bad habit and, like most bad habits, with a bit of willpower, you should be able to stop it.

Stop regressing

Another bad habit is 'regression'. No, not going back into your subconscious and discovering you were Cleopatra's favourite eunuch in a past life. When reading, regression is going back over text to check you read it right. Rather than consolidating understanding, this tends to break the flow of concentration and decreases your overall comprehension. Only go back if you really need to.

Use headings

Consider whether your text has any tools to help you speed up your reading. Are there lots of headings summarising contents, or bullet points for you to scan?

Use a finger

Don't feel you're too grown up to use a finger to trace your reading. It will help keep your eye focussed on precisely where you are in the text, increasing your pace.

Choose carefully

Accept that some documentation does not lend itself to speed reading. If you're signing off on a mortgage, for instance, don't be tempted to take a shortcut on the small print. Similarly, a piece of delicately crafted verse by your one true love should not be read like a set of revision notes.

Armed with this information, have a go at the following exercise.

Quiz 6 – Speed Reading

In this extract from 'The Red-Headed League', Jabez Wilson, a pawnbroker by trade, is reporting to Holmes a conversation he had with one Duncan Ross, who proposes to employ Wilson in a rather extraordinary position. The passage is 250 words long. Give yourself just thirty seconds to read it, then turn over the page and answer a series of questions to see how much you absorbed.

'What would be the hours?' I asked.

'Ten to two.'

Now a pawnbroker's business is mostly done of an evening, Mr. Holmes, especially Thursday and Friday evening, which is just before payday; so it would suit me very well to earn a little in the mornings. Besides, I knew that my assistant was a good man, and that he would see to anything that turned up.

'That would suit me very well,' said I. 'And the pay?'

'Is four pounds a week.'

'And the work?'

'Is purely nominal.'

'What do you call purely nominal?'

'Well, you have to be in the office, or at least in the building, the whole time. If you leave, you forfeit your whole position forever. The will is very clear upon that point. You don't comply with the conditions if you budge from the office during that time.'

'It's only four hours a day, and I should not think of leaving,' said I.

'No excuse will avail,' said Mr. Duncan Ross; 'neither sickness nor business nor anything else. There you must stay, or you lose your billet.'

'And the work?'

'Is to copy out the Encyclopedia Britannica. There is the first volume of it in that press. You must find your own ink, pens, and blotting-paper, but we provide this table and chair. Will you be ready tomorrow?'

'Certainly,' I answered.

'Then, good-bye, Mr. Jabez Wilson, and let me congratulate you once more on the important position which you have been fortunate enough to gain.'

Questions

1. How much does Ross propose to pay Wilson?
2. Which famous work is Wilson to copy out?
3. What hours is Wilson expected to work?
4. What tools must Wilson provide for himself?
5. When is most business at a pawnbroker's shop done, according to Wilson?

Keeping an Open Mind

'The more bizarre a thing is the less mysterious it proves to be. It is your commonplace, featureless crimes which are really puzzling, just as a commonplace face is the most difficult to identify.'
'THE RED-HEADED LEAGUE'

In sporting parlance, Holmes was extremely adept at playing what was in front of him. That is to say, whatever plans he may have had up his sleeve, he would alter them to suit the scenario in which he found himself. No matter how odd or surprising a situation became, he kept his mind open to all sorts of extraordinary possibilities. He realised that just because something seemed unlikely, it was not impossible. Such flexibility of thinking was crucial to his solving many a case.

For us mere mortals, having our presumptions knocked to pieces can be an extremely disconcerting experience and throws many of us off kilter, rendering us unable to deal with a new situation or to process a new piece of information. We are so sure that we are right about so many things that the possibility we may actually be wrong about them is all but inconceivable to us.

History throws up plenty of examples of lack of open-mindeness. Galileo had a very serious falling-out with the Roman Catholic Church over his insistence that the Earth revolves around the sun and not the other way round – a proposition few would have trouble accepting today. Yet still we accept all sorts of ideas as irrefutable truth when, in fact, they are simply not true. Consider a few of these urban myths.

The Great Wall of China is the only man-made object on Earth visible from the moon. False – it is not visible from the moon.

President Kennedy told the German people that he was a jelly doughnut. False. It is true that in a 1963 speech he said 'Ich bin ein Berliner'. It is also true that there is a certain kind of doughnut called a Berliner. If, as it is often said he should have, Kennedy had said 'Ich bin Berliner', he would have been suggesting he was a native of the city, which he wasn't. His formulation was grammatically correct and put across his desired sentiment: he was at one with the people of Berlin.

To demonstrate the limitations of kingly power, Canute, the eleventh century King of England, commanded the sea to halt before it wet his feet. False. The story is almost certainly apocryphal.

Sherlock Holmes was real. He wasn't. Honestly. To be able to maintain openness of mind is a potent skill and requires of us that we do not spring to judgement or take things at face value, nor refuse to countenance that what we thought was one thing is actually another.

Thinking Laterally

'What is out of the common is usually a guide
rather than a hindrance.'
'A STUDY IN SCARLET'

In recent times the world has become filled with over-
paid and self-appointed consultants extolling the virtues
of 'blue sky thinking', 'pushing the envelope' and
'thinking outside the box'. For all its silliness, there is a
valid point hidden amidst their jargon. Simply put, an
ability to think laterally – to look at a problem from
many different angles rather than blundering into it
head-on – can be a richly rewarding enterprise.

Holmes was an undeniable master of lateral
thinking. Virtually every case written up by Dr Watson
involves Holmes making a dextrous intellectual leap
that no-one else proves capable of. Your chances of
matching Holmes in feats of lateral thinking are, quite
frankly, minimal. You might as well decide you can out-
dribble Lionel Messi, talk about string theory more
convincingly than Stephen Hawking, or wear

something weirder than Lady Gaga. Some talents are bestowed on just a few, and when it comes to lateral thinking, no one touches Holmes.

Yet that should not stop you from developing your skills in this direction as far as you possibly can. Here are a few quizzes to get the cogs whirring.

Quiz 7 – Lost for Words

In this exercise, add a word in Column B that makes two new words when added to the end of the word in Column A and to the beginning of the word in Column C. (If you prefer, write your answers, in order, on a sheet of paper.)

A	B	C
break	Out	standing
honey	MOON	beam
note	book	keeper
police		hole
stone		paper
screen		time

Quiz 8 – Dingbats

In this exercise, each of the following dingbats represents a different Sherlock Holmes story. Can you work out which each refers to? Write your answers on a separate sheet of paper.

1  **THE ROLLING STONES**

2 Bohe Profumomia

3 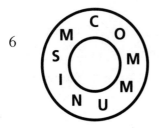 **AG**

4 **B^LO_K^E**

5 **Fred Astaire, Rudolf Nureyev, Nijinsky, Gene Kelly**

6 A circle with letters reading: C O M M U N I S M

7 Bonneparte, Boney, The Little Corporal, Corsican Ogre, Husband of Josephine, Emperor of the French

8 $$2-{}^1/_4=1?$$

9

10   Cu + Copacabana/Bondi/Venice

Quiz 9 – What Next?

In this quiz, attempt to complete each sequence by filling in the last two missing elements. There is a clear pattern behind each sequence but you will have to rack your brains to work out just what it is.

1. Genesis Exodus Leviticus Numbers Deuteronomy Joshua Judges Ruth _____ _____

2. M T W T F _S_ _S_

3. 31 28 31 30 31 30 31 31 30 31 __ __

4. M V E M J S __ __

5. A S D F G H J _K_ _L_

6. Moscow, Los Angeles, Seoul, Barcelona, Atlanta, Sydney, Athens, Beijing, _____, _____

Russia   Us   SK   US
aus

7. 1660 1685 1688 1702 1714 1727 1760 1820 1830 1837 1901 1910 _____ _____

8. Czech Republic, Slovakia, Eritrea, Palau, Timor Leste, Montenegro, _____, _____

(If necessary, write your answers on a separate sheet of paper)

Quiz 10 – What on Earth?

Some lateral-thinking teasers to tax you.

1. A man walks into a bar and asks for a glass of water. The barman goes to pour one when he suddenly lurches at the customer across the bar, letting rip a blood-curdling roar. The customer thanks the barman and leaves. Why?

2. Louise's father has three daughters. The oldest is called April and the next oldest is called May. What is the youngest called? Louise

3. Tom goes into Harry's shop and asks Harry how much a chocolate bar costs. Harry says it's sixty pence for one or a pound for two. Tom puts a pound down on the counter and Harry asks if he wants one or two bars. A few minutes later, Dick enters the shop and asks Harry the same question about price, receiving the same answer. Dick also puts a pound down on the counter

and Harry gives him two bars without asking
how many he wants. Why?

4. Is it legal for a woman to marry her widower's
   brother?

5. A French plane crashes in Luxembourg. Where
   should the survivors be buried?

6. A grove has three crates labelled 'Oranges',
   'Lemons' and 'Oranges & Lemons'. Each of the
   boxes is incorrectly labelled. How can you work
   out which label goes on which box by
   removing one piece of fruit from one box only?

7. Dodgy Don is suspected of theft from a
   company he has just been visiting. He is
   stopped by the police but they find nothing
   incriminating either on him or in the van he is
   driving. Nonetheless, the police arrest him and
   charge him with theft. What had he stolen?

The van?

Choosing Your Friends Wisely

'I confess, my dear fellow, that I am very much in your debt.'
'THE HOUND OF THE BASKERVILLES'

For all that Holmes stands alone as the greatest detective in English literature, he was but one half of a remarkable double act even though he was sometimes reluctant to admit it. Holmes was self-confident (even arrogant) and occasionally teased Watson mercilessly. Even when he was 'being nice', his compliments could be distinctly double-edged. In *The Hound of the Baskervilles*, he told Watson rather condescendingly: 'It may be that you are not yourself luminous, but you are a conductor of light. Some people without possessing genius have a remarkable power of stimulating it.'

Some portrayals in television and film productions

(notably Nigel Bruce's Watson alongside Basil Rathbone's Holmes in the Hollywood movies of the 1930s and 1940s), depicted Watson as a bungler. He was not. Here was a qualified doctor who had served his country in India and Afghanistan. He had foibles of his own (there are numerous suggestions of a historic over-fondness for alcohol and gambling), but in his partnership with Holmes he was never less than loyal and extraordinarily brave, and often provided that dose of humanity lacking in the Great Detective.

Holmes knew this too. When he baited Watson, it was usually done with the mischievous affection common to strong male friendships. Holmes had the insight to recognise that Watson filled some of the gaps in his own personality and was the perfect ally whenever he was needed. Watson was Holmes's 'someone … on whom I can thoroughly rely'. During their Baskerville adventure, Sherlock admitted that 'There is no man who is better worth having at your side when you are in a tight place'.

Crucially, Watson was also an impeccable foil for Holmes, someone with whom the Great Detective could discuss his train of thought (though he often did so in an infuriatingly enigmatic manner). Holmes even stated: 'Nothing clears up a case so much as stating it to another person.' If there were gaps in his thinking, talking over his deductions with Watson was a sure way to expose them.

Watson in his turn understood what he brought to the crime-fighting party. 'I was a whetstone for his mind,' he wrote in 'The Adventure of the Creeping Man'. 'I stimulated him.' In 'His Last Bow', a troubled Holmes told his old friend: 'Good old Watson! You are the one fixed point in a changing age.' But perhaps Holmes summed it up best in 'The Adventure of the Dying Detective': 'You won't fail me. You never did fail me.'

Holmes, a man who by his own admission had 'never loved', knew that, in the words of John Donne, 'no man is an island'. He understood that a trusted friendship did not lessen him or steal glory away from him but made him more than he otherwise would have been. He would, no doubt, have agreed with the seventeenth-century English poet Abraham Cowley:

Acquaintance I would have, but when it depends
Not on the number, but the choice of friends.

Accepting Good Fortune

'We have certainly been favoured with
extraordinary good luck.'
'THE ADVENTURE OF THE BERYL CORONET'

It is easy to assume that Sherlock's great mind
guaranteed success in his cases but he was subject to
luck – good and bad – just like the rest of us. In 'The
Adventure of Black Peter', the case was solved 'simply
by having the good fortune to get the right clue from
the beginning.' Alternatively, in *The Hound of the
Baskervilles*, Watson talked of how 'Luck had been

against us again and again in this enquiry, but now at last it came to my aid.'

None of us can control the influence of good fortune on our lives but it may just be possible to tip the odds in our favour. In 2003, Professor Richard Wiseman revealed the results of his ten-year study into good and bad luck. His findings suggested that 'lucky' people generate their own good luck. He wrote in the *Daily Telegraph*:

> My research revealed that lucky people generate good fortune via four basic principles. They are skilled at creating and noticing chance opportunities, make lucky decisions by listening to their intuition, create self-fulfilling prophesies via positive expectations, and adopt a resilient attitude that transforms bad luck into good.

Wiseman is not the first authority to suggest that we can influence our own fortune. Ovid wrote, 'Luck, affects everything; let your hook always be cast; in the stream where you least expect it, there will be a fish.' The great movie mogul Samuel Goldwyn noted 'The harder I work, the luckier I get.'

There is anecdotal evidence, too, that great things can spring from a slice of good luck. Everything from Christopher Columbus stumbling upon America while searching for a new eastern passage, to Alexander Fleming's discovery of penicillin and even the invention of Coca-Cola, all owed a great deal to good fortune.

In short, if good fortune chooses to search you out, do not reject it. Embrace it. Sherlock Holmes certainly did when it came around.

Learning From Your Mistakes

'I made a blunder, my dear Watson – which is, I am afraid, a more common occurrence than anyone would think who only knew me through your memoirs.'
'SILVER BLAZE'

Everybody makes mistakes. Even the Great Detective. But he knew that to make a mistake is forgivable so long as you make it only once. Consider his comments on the subject in 'The Disappearance of Lady Frances Carfax':

'Should you care to add the case to your annals, my dear Watson,' said Holmes that evening, 'it can only be as an example of that temporary eclipse to which even the best-balanced mind may be exposed. Such slips are common to all mortals, and the greatest is he who can recognise and repair them. To this modified credit I may, perhaps, make some claim.'

Today, making a mistake is considered an integral factor in progressing and developing. In 2007, Robert Sutton, a professor of management science and engineering at Stanford University, wrote a blog for the Harvard Business Review:

> One of the mottoes that Diego Rodriguez and I use at the Stanford d.school (Institute of Design) is 'failure sucks, but instructs'. We encourage students to learn from the constant stream of small setbacks and successes that are produced by doing things (rather than just talking about what to do). To paraphrase our d.school founder and inspiration David Kelley: 'If you keep making the same mistakes again and again, you aren't learning anything. If you keep making new and different mistakes, that means you are doing new things and learning new things.'

Keeping Focus

'My mind is like a racing engine, tearing itself to pieces because it is not connected up with the work for which it was built.'
'THE ADVENTURE OF WISTERIA LODGE'

As your old school teachers wearied of drumming into you as a child, the best way to avoid making mistakes is to maintain concentration. As Watson recorded in 'The Adventure of the Solitary Cyclist', Holmes 'loved above all things precision and concentration of thought'.

For most of us, our minds are in a state of flux. We keep a lot of stuff in our heads and too easily we can fall into the trap of turning it over to no real advantage. Without a bit of focus we might find ourselves utterly submerged beneath the chaos going on in our skulls.

Yet somehow most of us maintain a degree of control over our thought processes by concentrating on whatever needs to be concentrated on at any given moment. Quite how we do this as effectively as we do is something of a mystery which some of the greatest minds alive today are attempting to solve. What they broadly agree on is that, as a species, we have a remarkable propensity for 'attentional control'. Here are a few suggestions as to how to improve your concentration:

As with keeping your brain agile, your ability to concentrate is directly related to how rested, relaxed and well-fuelled you are. If you know that you need your concentration levels to be at their best, make sure you are eating and drinking well, getting a good night's sleep and are incorporating some relaxation time into your schedule.

If you need a burst of concentration, a shot of caffeine might do the trick, though research suggests the more regularly you drink it, the less effective it becomes.

Keep things fresh. It is easy to slip into dull routine but boredom is a sure-fire way to lose focus. It is far more likely you will slip up at work if you're doing the same process for the thousandth time while you stare out of the window, wishing you were somewhere more exciting. If you feel yourself drifting off, take a moment to do or plan something that actually interests you – afterwards, you will likely find yourself better able to focus on the immediate job in hand.

Don't multitask excessively. It is said by some that this is never a problem for the male of the species as he has an innate inability to multitask. But no-one is really at their best if they are doing seventy-three different things at once. If you really need to focus on an activity, give it your undivided attention.

Put yourself in a place where there aren't a multitude of distractions.

Train yourself to consciously concentrate when you need to. Tell yourself 'I need to concentrate now' (or something similar) if it helps you to focus.

Work out when your best concentrating time is. Some of us are early birds, others are night owls and still others find they're most productive just after lunch. Work out when your optimum hours are and schedule in tasks that require the highest levels of concentration in these periods.

Another useful tactic is to do activities and play games that promote concentration. Here are a few ideas to get you started:

Say the alphabet backwards. When you've done it once, do it again but quicker.

Recall all the countries you have ever visited.

List the birthdays of everyone in your family.

Remember everybody from your class at school.

Do your times tables. Not just the easy ones, but the ones that always trip you up.

Choose a subject of particular interest to you and test yourself on it. For instance, if you're obsessed with The Beatles, try to name all of their number one hits. Or if you're fanatical about football, name the champions for each season as far back as you can remember.

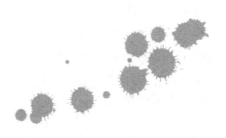

Logic and Deduction

'I never guess. It is a shocking habit – destructive to
the logical faculty.'
'THE SIGN OF FOUR'

Holmes's remarkable faculties are shown at their best
time and again when he is making deductions from
evidence that seems to the rest of us to yield little of
value. Indeed, so accurate are the conclusions he draws
that at times it seems almost as if he has mystical powers
or psychic abilities. But what is the process of logical
deduction?

Accumulate evidence.
By using his finely-honed powers of observation,
Holmes was able to gather vast amounts of
information from even the most unpromising of
sources.

Ask the right questions.

Holmes formulated clear questions in his head that he wished to answer. For instance, what does this person's clothing tell me about where they come from or what sort of job they have? What does a dog's silence signify? Why might a red-headed pawnbroker be required to copy out an encyclopaedia for several hours a day?

Formulate hypotheses.

Consider an otherwise well-dressed doctor who arrives at Baker Street carrying a rugged walking cane and wearing shoes covered in compacted mud of a colour not usual in the capital. Why might this be? Does he not look after his shoes properly? Are London's shoeshine boys on strike? Has he come in a hurry from an appointment in the country?

Evaluate hypotheses.

The doctor is smartly dressed so it is unlikely that he simply doesn't pay attention to his shoes. You went out for a walk earlier and saw a shoeshine boy so you know they are not on strike. The doctor does seem flustered, however, as if he has rushed to Baker Street.

Reach a conclusion.
Ask the doctor what has caused him to hurry away from his rural practice.

On the occasion of Watson's very first meeting with Holmes in *A Study in Scarlet*, the Great Detective gives a master class in logical deduction. Watson had arrived in London looking for lodgings and Holmes was searching for someone with whom to share rooms, so the two men were introduced by a mutual friend named Stamford:

'Dr. Watson, Mr. Sherlock Holmes,' said Stamford, introducing us.

'How are you?' he said cordially, gripping my hand with a strength for which I should hardly have given him credit.

'You have been in Afghanistan, I perceive.'

'How on earth did you know that?' I asked in astonishment.

'Never mind,' said he, chuckling to himself. 'The

question now is about haemoglobin. No doubt you see the significance of this discovery of mine?'

And so the story progresses. The two men agree to take rooms together and Holmes eventually divulges to his new companion just how he achieved such a remarkable insight:

I knew you came from Afghanistan. From long habit the train of thoughts ran so swiftly through my mind, that I arrived at the conclusion without being conscious of intermediate steps. There were such steps, however. The train of reasoning ran, 'Here is a gentleman of a medical type, but with the air of a military man. Clearly an army doctor, then. He has just come from the tropics, for his face is dark, and that is not the natural tint of his skin, for his wrists are fair. He has undergone hardship and sickness, as his haggard face says clearly. His left arm has been injured. He holds it in a stiff and unnatural manner. Where in the tropics could an English army doctor have seen much hardship and got his arm wounded? Clearly in Afghanistan.' The whole train of thought did not occupy a second. I then remarked that you came from Afghanistan, and you were astonished.

Conan Doyle took his inspiration for such deductive brilliance from a real-life source: Dr Joseph Bell. Conan Doyle studied medicine at Edinburgh University under Bell in the 1870s and would later write to tell him, 'It is certainly to you that I owe Sherlock Holmes... I do not think that his analytical work is in the least an exaggeration of some effects which I have seen you produce in the out-patient ward.'

Bell's great trick was to diagnose a patient and discern his background without taking any form of history. It was said he could spot a sailor by his rolling gait, a traveller's route by the tattoos he bore, and any number of occupations from a glimpse at a subject's hands. As if to prove the point, Conan Doyle once saw him correctly place a patient as a non-commissioned officer, recently discharged from the Highland Regiment posted in Barbados.

In *A Study in Scarlet*, Watson arose one morning to find a magazine on the table of 221B Baker Street. His eye was drawn to one particular article bearing a pencil mark at the heading:

Its somewhat ambitious title was 'The Book of Life', and it attempted to show how much an observant man might learn by an accurate and systematic examination of all that came in his way. It struck me as being a remarkable mixture of shrewdness and of absurdity. The reasoning was close and intense, but the deductions appeared to me to be far fetched and exaggerated. The writer claimed by a momentary expression, a twitch of a muscle or a glance of an eye, to fathom a man's inmost thoughts. Deceit, according to him, was an impossibility in the case of one trained to observation and analysis. His conclusions were as infallible as so many propositions of Euclid. So startling would his results appear to the uninitiated that until they learned the processes by which he had arrived at them they might well consider him as a necromancer.

Watson was initially rather dismissive of its contents, describing it as 'ineffable twaddle' and claiming not to have 'read such rubbish in my life'. A moment or two later, though, Holmes revealed that he himself was the author of the piece. As such, it is invaluable to students of the Great Detective for its explanation of his deductive process:

'From a drop of water,' said the writer, 'a logician could infer the possibility of an Atlantic or a Niagara without having seen or heard of one or the other. So all life is a great chain, the nature of which is known whenever we are shown a single link of it. Like all other arts, the Science of Deduction and Analysis is one which can only be acquired by long and patient study, nor is life long enough to allow any mortal to attain the highest possible perfection in it. Before turning to those moral and mental aspects of the matter which present the greatest difficulties, let the inquirer begin by mastering more elementary problems. Let him, on meeting a fellow-mortal, learn at a glance to distinguish the history of the man, and the trade or profession to which he belongs. Puerile as such an exercise may seem, it sharpens the faculties of observation, and teaches one where to look and what to look for. By a man's fingernails, by his coat-sleeve, by his boots, by his trouser-knees, by the callosities of his forefinger and thumb, by his expression, by his shirtcuffs -- by each of these things a man's calling is plainly revealed. That all united should fail to enlighten the competent inquirer in any case is almost inconceivable.'

'Yes; I have a turn both for observation and for deduction,' Holmes told Watson. 'The theories which I have expressed there, and which appear to you to be so chimerical, are really extremely practical – so practical that I depend upon them for my bread and cheese.'

Improving Your Deductive Skills

"'When I hear you give your reasons," I remarked,
"the thing always appears to me to be so
ridiculously simple that I could easily do it myself,
though at each successive instance of your
reasoning I am baffled until you explain your
process.'"
'A SCANDAL IN BOHEMIA'

To improve your own deductive powers, you can do no
better than read the entire Sherlock Holmes canon.
School yourself in the many incredible examples of
deductive reasoning that litter the stories and aim to
mirror as many of the master's techniques as humanly
possible. To watch the Great Detective in action is never
less than a delight, as Watson himself recalled in 'The
Adventure of the Speckled Band':

I had no keener pleasure than in following Holmes in his
professional investigations, and in admiring the rapid
deductions, as swift as intuitions, and yet always founded

on a logical basis with which he unravelled the problems
which were submitted to him.

There are far too many examples to cite here, but
virtually anything could serve as useful evidence for
Holmes. Here was a man who could discern vast
amounts about a suspect from the cigar ash he left
scattered at a crime scene, who could calculate a man's
height from the implied stride length provided by a set
of footprints, and who could even (in 'The Adventure
of the Beryl Coronet') unravel 'a very long and
complex story ... written in the snow in front of me'.

There are one or two grand set pieces worth
analysing in the pursuit of learning Holmes's secrets.
The Sign of Four offers up a particularly notable
example. Watson hands Holmes a pocket watch and
challenges Sherlock to provide 'an opinion upon the
character or habits of the late owner'. Holmes begins by
complaining that the watch has recently been cleaned,
robbing him of his best evidence. This is, as we might
suspect, simply a bit of showmanship on his part.

'Subject to your correction, I should judge that the watch belonged to your elder brother, who inherited it from your father,' he begins.

'That you gather, no doubt, from the H. W. upon the back?' Watson fires back.

'Quite so. The W. suggests your own name. The date of the watch is nearly fifty years back, and the initials are as old as the watch: so it was made for the last generation. Jewellery usually descends to the eldest son, and he is most likely to have the same name as the father. Your father has, if I remember right, been dead many years. It has, therefore, been in the hands of your eldest brother.'

So far, so logical. But then comes a leap in Holmes's deductions that at first sight seems beyond reasonable:

He was a man of untidy habits, - very untidy and careless. He was left with good prospects, but he threw away his chances, lived for some time in poverty with occasional short intervals of prosperity, and finally, taking to drink, he died. That is all I can gather.

Initially, Watson is knocked back on his haunches, distraught that such a painful personal episode has been so casually revealed. He accuses Holmes of being 'unworthy', suggesting he had made prior enquiries into his family's past or else had resorted to guess work. Holmes soon corrects his companion:

What seems strange to you is only so because you do not follow my train of thought or observe the small facts upon which large inferences may depend. For example, I began by stating that your brother was careless. When you observe the lower part of that watch-case you notice that it is not only dinted in two places, but it is cut and marked all over from the habit of keeping other hard objects, such as coins or keys, in the same pocket. Surely it is no great feat to assume that a man who treats a fifty-guinea watch so cavalierly must be a careless man. Neither is it a very far-fetched inference that a man who inherits one article of such value is pretty well provided for in other respects.

It is very customary for pawnbrokers in England, when they take a watch, to scratch the number of the ticket with a pin-point upon the inside of the case. It is more handy than a label, as there is no risk of the number being lost or transposed. There are no less than four such numbers visible to my lens on the inside of this case. Inference - that your brother was often at low water. Secondary inference, - that he had occasional bursts of prosperity, or he could not have redeemed the pledge. Finally, I ask you to look at the inner plate, which contains the key-hole. Look at the thousands of scratches all round the hole, - marks where the key has slipped. What sober man's key could have scored those grooves? But you will never see a drunkard's watch without them. He winds it at night, and he leaves these traces of his unsteady hand.

What you can't learn about deduction from the Holmes stories is probably not worth knowing, but here are a few other hints and tips to help:

We all make deductions every day. If we turn on a light switch but no light comes on, we deduce that we need to put in a new light bulb or there is a problem with the electrics. And if we get to the railway station at rush hour and see an empty platform, we might well deduce that a train has just gone or there are no trains running. At the heart of logical deduction is an ability to make leaps of the imagination. Break the process down into manageable stages.

The more evidence, the better you can test out a hypothesis.

The devil is in the detail. It is very often the tiniest details that give away the biggest truths.

Trust in your intuition, but only up to a point. 'It was easier to know it than to explain why I know it,' Holmes said on one occasion. 'If you were asked to prove that two and two made four, you might find some difficulty, and yet you are quite sure of the fact.' However, it is always well to subject your intuitions to thorough analysis to make sure that what you believe to be a fact is not merely a heartfelt conviction not borne out by the evidence.

Don't allow your deductive reasoning to be clouded by your personal feelings or prejudices.

Fit your theories to the facts. Do not fit the facts to your theories. In the first instance, you are reading the evidence. In the latter, you are rewriting the evidence simply to accord with your own preconceived ideas.

Beware of the 'conjunction fallacy'. This is when two or more events that could happen together or separately are considered more likely to happen together than separately. A classic example was provided in a study by the psychologists Amos Tversky and Daniel Kahneman. They provided respondents with the following description: 'Linda is thirty-one years old, single, outspoken, and very bright. She majored in philosophy. As a student, she was deeply concerned with issues of discrimination and social justice, and also participated in anti-nuclear demonstrations.' They then asked their respondents which was the more probable scenario: 1) Linda is a bank teller, or 2) Linda is a bank teller and is active in the feminist movement. Eighty-five per cent of respondents went for the second option but by the laws of probability, the answer must be the first.

Just because your conclusion seems odd, even incredible, does not mean it's wrong. As Holmes noted in 'A Case of Identity': 'Life is infinitely stranger than anything which the mind of man could invent.' Don't be embarrassed by the strangeness of a hypothesis if the evidence is there to support it.

Deduction is not a perfect science. Confirm your findings before sharing them. Joseph Bell once wrote: 'From close observation and deduction you can make a correct diagnosis of any and every case. However, never neglect to ratify your deductions.'

Logic and Deduction Exercises

Let's start with a classic logic grid problem. In this type of problem, there are a number of categories, each containing a number of different options. The aim is to find which of the options are linked together by utilising a series of clues. At first sight it may seem like the evidence does not provide you with sufficient information to reach the one unique solution, but everything you need is there. The grid allows you to cross-reference every possible option in each and every category. The things you know to be true, mark with a tick. Put a cross against those you know to be false. By using deduction, you will eventually find a solution.

Quiz 11 – Most Irregular

Holmes has sent five of the wiliest members of his Baker Street Irregulars to keep surveillance on a gang of bank robbers. Each Irregular must keep an eye on a suspect with a particular distinguishing feature, and each has been assigned to a particular stop on the London Metropolitan line (the stretch of railway line that runs from Baker Street through Portland Road, Gower Street and King's Cross before finishing at Farringdon Street). From the clues below, can you figure out what distinguishing feature each Irregular will be looking out for and where they have been sent? (Draw the grid on a sheet of paper if you need to.)

1. Wiggins is at Farringdon Street but his 'mark' doesn't have a scar on his chin.

2. The robber in the crumpled hat is being watched by the boy at Portland Road. The boy watching the suspect with red hair is at King's Cross but is not called Johnny.

3. Tommy, who is watching the criminal wearing trousers rolled up at the knee, is at the station immediately after Jimmy.

	Crumpled hat	Red hair	Scar on chin	Trousers rolled up	Wears a waistcoat	Baker Street	Portland Road	Gower Street	Kings Cross	Farringdon Street
Wiggins										
Smiffy										
Jimmy										
Tommy										
Johnny										
Baker Street										
Portland Road										
Gower Street										
Kings Cross										
Farringdon Street										

Quiz 12 – CSI Baker Street

Read through the following perplexing scenes of death. Using your powers of logic and lateral thinking, see if you can deduce what exactly has occurred in each case.

1. Professor Murray is found hanging in his study. There is no furniture near him but there is a puddle of water beneath his feet. What has happened? *He was killed while in the tub by a John Doe then strong up by said JD to look like a suicide.*

2. Kenny Adrenalin is discovered dead in the middle of the Sahara. He is face down in the sand, sporting a large backpack. There is no sign of foul play. *Perhaps the two brothers were thrown or perhaps those were their camels & suffered injuries/ severe mileage so Benny's nakedness suggest dehydration & helicopters*

3. Kenny's brother, Benny, is found dead in the same spot a month later. He too is lying in the sand, naked, with a length of straw in his hand.

4. Dave Wave, a scuba diver, is found dead in full

diving gear in the middle of a forest that has just witnessed ferocious fires. Dave, though, is unburned and the sea is thirty miles away.

5. A child wakes up and sadly notes the presence of some coal, a carrot and a scarf on the lawn. No one has placed them there. The boy's father says, 'What's up, son?' The boy replies, 'It's Bobby.' A tear catches in his eye. What has happened?

6. A man is slumped in the driver's seat of a car, a bullet wound to the back of his head. The murder weapon is stashed on the back passenger shelf, out of reach of the dead man. He is alone in the car, all the doors are locked and the windows up. What has happened?

II:
Building Your Knowledge Base

Knowing Your Subject

'It is a capital mistake to theorise before you have all the evidence. It biases the judgement.'
'A SCANDAL IN BOHEMIA'

Sherlock Holmes was a walking encyclopaedia, wasn't he? Surely he, of all men, could hold forth on pretty much any subject you cared to mention? The answers to these questions are not as clear-cut as you might expect. Take Watson's early impression of the breadth of Holmes's knowledge, as detailed in *A Study in Scarlet*:

His ignorance was as remarkable as his knowledge. Of contemporary literature, philosophy and politics he appeared to know next to nothing. Upon my quoting Thomas Carlyle, he inquired in the naivest way who he might be and what he had done. My surprise reached a climax, however, when I found incidentally that he was ignorant of the Copernican Theory and of the composition of the solar system. That any civilised human being in this nineteenth century should not be aware that the Earth travelled round the sun appeared to me to be such an extraordinary fact that I could hardly realise it.

In the same story, Watson gave this more detailed rundown of his new friend's areas of strength and weakness:

Sherlock Holmes - his limits

1. Knowledge of Literature. - Nil.
2. " " Philosophy. - Nil.
3. " " Astronomy. - Nil.
4. " " Politics. - Feeble.
5. " " Botany. - Variable. Well up in belladonna, opium, and poisons generally. Knows nothing of practical gardening.
6. Knowledge of Geology. - Practical, but limited. Tells at a glance different soils from each other. After walks has shown me splashes upon his trousers, and told me by their colour and consistence in what part of London he had received them.
7. Knowledge of Chemistry. - Profound.
8. " " Anatomy. - Accurate, but unsystematic.

9. "   " Sensational Literature. - Immense. He appears to know every detail of every horror perpetrated in the century.

10. Plays the violin well.

11. Is an expert singlestick player, boxer, and swordsman.

12. Has a good practical knowledge of British law.

Holmes played upon the alleged deficiencies in his knowledge at various times. In 'The Adventure of the Noble Bachelor', he insisted, 'I read nothing except the criminal news and the agony column'; when challenged on his ignorance of the solar system, he demanded of Watson: 'What the deuce is it to me?'

We should take all this with a pinch of salt. Holmes was focussed on the job at hand and he thus attempted to clear his mind of intellectual clutter irrelevant to a particular task. Knowledge for Holmes was purely utilitarian (something quite at odds with the Victorian era's love of knowledge for its own sake). 'Holmes is a little too scientific for my tastes,' Stamford told Watson before introducing him to Sherlock.

'It approaches to cold-bloodedness. I could imagine his giving a friend a little pinch of the latest vegetable alkaloid, not out of malevolence, you understand, but simply out of a spirit of inquiry in order to have an accurate idea of the effects. To do him justice, I think that he would take it himself with the same readiness. He appears to have a passion for definite and exact knowledge.'

Would knowledge of the solar system have assisted Holmes greatly in solving any of his cases? Unlikely. Do we really believe that he didn't have at least a rudimentary grasp of the structure of the solar system? Not really. In 'The Greek Interpreter' he talks with confidence on the 'causes of the changes of the obliquity of the ecliptic', suggesting Watson was rather off beam in assuming a lack of astronomical knowledge.

Then there is the assertion about his breadth of reading. Critic E. V. Knox noted that in the course of the stories we see Holmes 'quote Goethe twice, discuss miracle plays, comment on Richter, Hafiz and Horace, and remark of Athelney Jones: "He has occasional glimmerings of reason. *Il n'y a pas des sots si incommodes que ceux qui ont de l'esprit!*'" Elsewhere he mentions Tacitus, Flaubert, Thoreau and Petrarch. Hardly suggestive of 'nil' knowledge of literature.

Holmes was also an innovator in several academic areas. Among the literature he produced were monographs on different types of tobacco ash, the polyphonic motets of Lassus, ciphers, document-dating, tattoos, tracing footprints, and the impact of trade upon the form of the hand. To say nothing of his 'Book of Life' or his Practical Handbook of Bee Culture. 'You have an extraordinary genius for minutiae,' Watson told him once. Indeed.

In conclusion, despite Watson's occasionally disparaging words, the extent of Holmes's knowledge was almost certainly as vast as you might expect. Perhaps his greatest genius was to be able to streamline his knowledge in the moment so that whatever was swirling around in his mind had, in Conan Doyle's own words, 'real practical application to life'.

Quiz 13 – Holmes Trivia

Sherlock Holmes overcame innumerable challenges by arming himself with the necessary knowledge to do so. By reading this book, it is assumed that you want to think like Sherlock. But how much do you actually know about him? Test yourself with this quiz.

1. What was Dr Watson's first name?

   John

2. Which famous family of French painters was Sherlock related to?

3. Who introduced Sherlock Holmes and Dr Watson? *One of John's war colleagues*

4. What was Irene Adler's job?

5. What was the name of Dr Watson's wife whom he met in *The Sign of Four*?

6. Who was the 'Napoleon of crime'?

7. Where had Dr Watson qualified as a doctor?

The Netley

8. What is the name of Sherlock's brother?

Mycroft

9. At which Pall Mall club was this brother a member?

10. Where did Sherlock apparently fall to his death in 1891? *The Falls*

11. What was Sherlock's London address?

12. What job title did he give himself?

13. Where did he settle in his retirement?

14. Where did Sherlock famously keep his stash of tobacco?

15. Holmes donned two disguises in *A Scandal in Bohemia*. Can you name one of them?

16. In which county was Baskerville Hall?

17. Who was the leader of the Baker Street Irregulars?

18. Which story details Holmes's first criminal investigation?

19. What is unusual about 'The Adventure of the Blanched Soldier' and 'The Adventure of the Lion's Mane'?

20. Where did Dr Watson keep papers concerning Holmes's other cases?

Obtaining Data

"'Data! data! data!" he cried impatiently. "I can't make bricks without clay.'"
'THE ADVENTURE OF THE COPPER BEECHES'

In his pursuit of the data vital to his professional occupation, Holmes relied on three main sources: the wealth of information stored within his brain, clues specific to a particular case that he discovered 'in the field', and reference sources.

Let us start by talking about his skill as a gatherer of clues. In an age when forensic detective work was a relatively new phenomenon, Holmes could read a crime scene and rake it for evidence like no other. He was way ahead of his time in appreciating the use of fingerprints, footprints, bloodstains and the like, as well as the time-sensitive nature of evidence-gathering. Here we may conjure the classic image of Holmes as he 'whipped a tape measure and a large round magnifying glass from his pocket.' In this respect, he often found himself battling the plods from the official police, who were less sensitive to preserving evidence. In 'The Boscombe Valley Mystery', he exclaimed of the crime scene: 'Oh, how simple it would all have been had I been here before they came like a herd of buffalo and wallowed all over it.'

Thankfully, forensics plays a much greater role in modern detection work and the police are extremely well-drilled in its demands. While police forces around the world each have their own guidelines, here are a few general tips on how forensic investigators go about their work:

Approach a crime scene with caution. Be aware of potential dangers – such as the on-going presence of a criminal or dangerous substances. If there are any victims at the scene, they are the priority and you should seek out assistance for them in the first instance.

Secure the scene at the earliest opportunity (with rope or tape) to avoid contamination of evidence.

This may offer the best hope of retrieving key evidence. After an initial survey, log all potentially useful information.

If there are any witnesses, be sure to get their statements. Take a note of all comings and goings at the scene.

Document the position of potential pieces of evidence. If a camera is not to hand, make drawings or keep notes.

Bring in the relevant experts for jobs such as fingerprint sweeping or bloodstain analysis.

Any evidence to be taken away should be handled as delicately as possibly (hands should be gloved at all times). Each item of evidence must be individually bagged and labelled.

An official record of the crime scene investigation should be written up as quickly as possible and handed over (with a briefing where necessary) to the investigating officer in charge.

However closely you have read this book and feel you are prepared to follow in the Great Detective's footsteps, do not insert yourself into a criminal investigation. Leave it to the police!

Once Holmes had gleaned as much as he possibly could from a crime scene, he would often consolidate his investigation by further background research of his own. This sometimes manifested itself in the form of experimentation. Holmes was infamous (particularly with Mrs Hudson) for the 'malodorous experiments' he undertook in his rooms and he was also variously witnessed beating cadavers to learn how far bruises may be produced after death and attempting to 'transfix a pig' with a single blow.

Then there are his indexes and books of reference. Watson described how Holmes had 'a horror of destroying documents', and his book shelves must have bowed under the weight of all the documentation he retained and cross-referenced. Had he lived today, Holmes may have regarded the era of the internet and the all-seeing search engine as his personal paradise. We might only imagine his joy at the prospect of being able to locate virtually any piece of information by typing a few words on a keyboard.

But before we get carried away with the thought that we are somehow masters of an information age, be warned! In 2011, an article appeared in the journal *Science*, entitled 'Google Effects on Memory: Cognitive Consequences of Having Information at Our Fingertips'. It was authored by Betsy Sparrow, a psychologist at Columbia University, and reflected on the findings of a research project that she had co-led. She wrote:

> Since the advent of search engines, we are reorganizing the way we remember things … Our brains rely on the internet for memory in much the same way they rely on the memory of a friend, family member or co-worker. We remember less through knowing information itself than by knowing where the information can be found.

What her study discovered was that we are far more likely to retain in our memories information that could not easily be found on the internet. However, where information could be retrieved from the web, respondents remembered how they could find that information again (e.g. through typing in a specific web address or search term) rather than the information itself. It is rather like remembering the name of a specific file within a particular filing cabinet, rather than the pertinent information within the file.

In truth, this is not as modern a phenomenon as we might assume. In the fourth century BC, Plato wrote *The Phaedrus*, in which Socrates is depicted narrating the tale of Thamus, an Egyptian king who hosted the god Theuth, among whose many achievements was said to be the invention of writing. Socrates spoke thus:

> You, who are the father of writing, have out of fondness
> for your offspring attributed to it quite the opposite of its
> real function. Those who acquire it will cease to exercise
> their memory and become forgetful; they will rely on
> writing to bring things to their remembrance by external
> signs instead of by their own internal resources. What
> you have discovered is a receipt for recollection, not for
> memory.
> (TRANSLATED BY WALTER HAMILTON, PENGUIN, 1973)

Quiz 14 – Elementary, dear reader ... Part I

Uriah Ingram is chief suspect in the grisly 'Limehouse
Butcher's Hook Murders'. It is known he is hiding out
in a parade of houses on the Commercial Road, though
the police do not know exactly which property. There
are houses numbered one to ninety-six on the road.
The police ask their informant three questions:

Is the number of the house below fifty?
Is the number divisible by three?
Is the number a square number?

The informant's answers are not recorded but we do know he would only answer exactly what he was asked and refused to divulge any further information. Nonetheless, the investigating officers knew from his answers Ingram's precise location and promptly arrested the killer. So where was Ingram holed up?

Reading the Signs

"'I have seen those symptoms before," said
Holmes, throwing his cigarette into the fire.
"Oscillation upon the pavement always means
an *affaire de coeur*."'
'A CASE OF IDENTITY'

It is difficult to overestimate the importance of body
language in our day-to-day dealings with the world.
Albert Mehrabian, Professor Emeritus of Psychology at
UCLA, argues that there are three major components
in face-to-face communication: words, tone of voice
and non-verbal communication. Of these, he rates
verbal communication as the least important aspect
(accounting for seven per cent of communication), then
tone of voice (thirty-eight per cent) and, finally, body
language (fifty-five per cent).

Body language encompasses gestures, facial
expressions (the eyes, it is said, are a window to the
soul), the positioning of the body and the proximity
between subjects, interaction with objects (e.g. a

cigarette or a pen) and even physical signs such as sweating or rate of breathing.

Becoming an adept reader of non-verbal communication and, consequently, more aware of your own body language gives you an advantage in all walks of life, whether socialising, in a professional context, in matters of the heart, or even facing-off across the card table.

Body language may not be the exact science of the type Holmes most enjoyed but he was nonetheless extravagantly adept at it. After all, this was a man whose greatness lay in his almost superhuman ability to read signs. This ability was never more evident than in his off-the-cuff analyses of his prospective clients, in which he would draw conclusions long before they had muttered a word. Consider the evidence presented by Watson in 'A Case of Identity':

He had risen from his chair and was standing between the parted blinds gazing down into the dull neutral-tinted London street. Looking over his shoulder, I saw that on the pavement opposite there stood a large woman with a heavy fur boa round her neck, and a large curling red feather in a broad-brimmed hat which was tilted in a coquettish Duchess of Devonshire fashion over her ear. From under this great panoply she peeped up in a nervous, hesitating fashion at our windows, while her body oscillated backward and forward, and her fingers fidgeted with her glove buttons. Suddenly, with a plunge, as of the swimmer who leaves the bank, she hurried across the road, and we heard the sharp clang of the bell.

'I have seen those symptoms before,' said Holmes, throwing his cigarette into the fire. 'Oscillation upon the pavement always means an affaire de coeur. She would like advice, but is not sure that the matter is not too delicate for communication. And yet even here we may discriminate. When a woman has been seriously wronged by a man she no longer oscillates, and the usual symptom is a broken bell wire. Here we may take it that there is a love matter, but that the maiden is not so much angry as perplexed, or grieved. But here she comes in person to resolve our doubts.'

'The Blanched Soldier' contains another scene in which Holmes (narrating himself on this occasion) presents a character with an assertion about a rather delicate matter. Note Holmes's close reading of his subject's body language:

> He stared at the writing with a face from which every expression save amazement had vanished.
>
> 'How do you know?' he gasped, sitting down heavily in his chair.
>
> 'It is my business to know things. That is my trade.'
>
> He sat in deep thought, his gaunt hand tugging at his straggling beard. Then he made a gesture of resignation.

The interpretation of body language is not something that may be learned overnight. It is a skill to be developed over a lifetime, your increasing experience of the world honing your abilities. Yet even after a lifetime, you cannot expect to be correct in your assumptions all of the time. In forming opinions of people, it is a tool that must only be used in conjunction with a great many other factors.

Let's start with a few basic things to consider when reading body language:

Context

A sign can have a multitude of meanings. If a gent is chatting to a young lady in a bar and she is constantly playing with her hair, it might well be that her action is unconsciously flirtatious. If she does the same thing in a job interview, it is more likely a sign of nervousness. Similarly, crossing your arms tight against yourself can, in many contexts, give away your sense of defensiveness. But if you're doing it in an igloo, it simply indicates that you're cold.

Culture

Certain actions have different meanings in different parts of the world. For instance, in Bulgaria, a nod of the head means 'no' and a shake means 'yes', a reversal of the custom followed in most other places. Similarly, in many parts of the world, an innocent 'thumbs-up' gesture can get you into an awful lot of trouble (for reasons that will go unexplained here in the interests of good taste).

Clusters

Read body language in clusters of consistent symbols to make the most effective reading. Just as taking a single word out of context from a sentence might leave you confused or thoroughly misled, so will reading non-verbal signs in isolation.

The simplest way to become better at reading body language is to practise. Keep an eye out for signals in your own interactions but watch others too. Sitting in a café for an hour and watching how the other customers interact with each other – the displays of affection, the temper tantrums, the seething resentments and complex power plays – can be a most instructive experience.

Here are a few useful tips to bear in mind when studying body language. Remember, these are necessarily generalities, not hard and fast rules. Indeed, some people will deliberately manipulate their own body language to mislead you. This list is but the tiniest tip of a vast iceberg:

Different sides of the brain deal with different functions. In simplistic terms, the right side deals with emotions and creativity and the left with facts and memories. If you ask someone a question and they look to the right, this may be an indication that they are fabricating or guessing. Looking to the left is indicative of fact retrieval.

Direct eye contact implies honesty, interest and even attraction. Dilated pupils and widened eyes may also be a signal of attraction, while excessive blinking is suggestive of nervousness or excitement. Making 'doe eyes' by looking up and sideways (especially when done by a female) suggests both vulnerability interest in a subject. Holding eye contact for an extended moment then looking away can be another signal of attraction.

A full-bodied, genuine laugh is indicative of a relaxed subject, but a tight-lipped smile is more likely to mean they are keeping something back.

Male posturing such as standing with chest out and shoulders back can be a sign of aggression or an attempt to capture female attention.

Nervous ticks include nail-biting, trembling hands and activities such as fiddling with a pen.

A raised chin is indicative of confidence and sometimes defiance (hence admonitions to 'keep your chin up' when the chips are down).

Crossed arms suggest defensiveness, as does the use of a prop such as a bag as a barrier between two subjects.

Touching or scratching the nose while speaking is sometimes suggestive that the subject is lying. Touching an ear while speaking might indicate indecisiveness.

Playing with hair can be a sign of flirtation or, conversely, a symptom of exasperation.

Handshakes can tell you much. A handshake in which both of a subject's hands are used implies they want to be trusted by the recipient of the handshake. A palm-up handshake suggests an element of submission, while a palm-down shake is a sign of wishing to dominate.

Leg direction while sitting. The feet and legs tend to point toward a subject of interest and away from one that is uninteresting or unwanted.

The mirroring of body language between two subjects is indicative of empathy, while non-synchronisation suggests the opposite. But mirroring should not be consciously forced, as it can appear as mockery.

Remember that while you are watching someone else's body language, they will be picking up signals from you too. Body language is a dialogue.

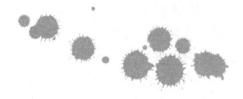

Laying Your Cards on the Table

'He had played nearly every day at one club or other, but he was a cautious player, and usually rose a winner.'
'THE ADVENTURE OF THE EMPTY HOUSE'

It is unclear how much of body language is inborn in us and how much is learned. Charles Darwin highlighted certain facial expressions (happiness, sadness, fear, disgust, surprise and anger) that are recognised across cultures, suggesting they at least are genetically inherited. But much else is learned socially.

The card table is one of the prime battlefields of body language. Every serious card player aims to mask their own body language, while attempting to discern the 'innate' body language of their opponents (i.e. that which cannot be masked). In this context, signals that indicate the hand of a player are known as 'tells'. The aim of a great player is to perfect the 'poker face', that serene look which gives nothing away to the onlooker.

There are plenty of characters in the Holmes stories who would have benefitted from this talent. Several men found themselves in all types of trouble (including virtual ruination) as a result of their lack of success at the gambling table (whist was seemingly the most common route to downfall in Sherlock's England). Watson himself had a tendency to gamble dangerously, to the extent that Holmes kept the good doctor's cheque book locked up for him. Here are a few tips regarding 'tells' that those players never learned:

Watch the face

This is where a trained eye can spot 'micro gestures' that are hard to control. If the eyes smile, they probably have a good hand. Many pros wear hats and glasses to hide these micro signals.

Check out how a player stacks their chips

As a very broad rule, a player who keeps an untidy stack is likely to play a loose game. A neat stack suggests a more conservative player. Surreptitious glancing at their chips suggests an opponent is preparing an attack.

Posture

Leaning back into a chair in a relaxed but upright manner can indicate relief or confidence. Conversely, hunching forward can indicate nervousness. Some card players claim that a rapidly jiggling knee beneath the table is the surest sign that someone thinks they have a winning hand.

> **Beware!**
> It is an integral part of the game that many players will consciously reverse their natural body language to confuse you. They will try to 'play it cool' if they have a good hand or appear super confident if they want to bluff with a weak hand. The trick is to work out exactly who is bluffing who.

Quiz 15 – Elementary, dear reader ... Part II

A smart London gent, Sir Sidney Welloff, has been set upon by a footpad, who violently relieved him of his purse containing a crisp five-pound note. Inspector Sniffemout of the Yard tracks down a band of four rogues, all drinking together at a tavern near Seven Dials. Sniffemout is sure one of them is guilty and, fortunately, knows there is not much honour among these thieves. He thinks they'll drop the guilty party in it if he only asks them the right question.

'So which one of you rogues robbed the gent, then?' asks the Inspector. They reply as follows:

Tom Dipper: It was Jack Hands.

Jack Hands: It was Joe Stealth, more like.

Billy Goldfingers: Well, it definitely weren't me, guv.

Joe Stealth: Jack Hands is telling you porkies, Inspector.

One of this likely lot is telling the truth, but only one. So who robbed Sir Sidney Welloff?

Mastering Disguise

'Accustomed as I was to my friend's amazing
powers in the use of disguises...'
'A SCANDAL IN BOHEMIA'

There were times when Holmes recognised that his
best chance of garnering crucial information was to go
undercover. This was no hardship for the Great
Detective. As he admitted in *The Valley of Fear*: 'Some
touch of the artist wells up within me, and calls
insistently for a well-staged performance.' Over the
course of his literary life, Sherlock was disguised as an
old seadog, an opium addict (a disguise so successful
that much of the world associates him with that
particular drug rather than his cocaine of choice), two
men of the cloth, a groom, a bookseller and a plumber.

Perhaps his most successful ruse was when he
managed to travel his way around large parts of the
world over a period of months or possibly years in the
guise of a Norwegian explorer named Sigerson. The
quasi-Scandinavian's exploits even found their way into

the press. So what made Holmes such a master of disguise? The answer is surely his utter commitment to assuming a role. Watson said as much in 'A Scandal in Bohemia': 'It was not merely that Holmes changed his costume. His expression, his manner, his very soul seemed to vary with every fresh part that he assumed. The stage lost a fine actor, even as science lost an acute reasoner, when he became a specialist in crime.'

Sherlock was a man who embraced method acting long before Brando, De Niro and the like. So how can you 'become' a character like Holmes?

Get the look.
When Holmes took on a disguise, he was preparing to enter the battlefield. To be discovered was to be at serious personal risk. As such, 'fancy dress' was never on the agenda and nor should it be for you. In particular, a badly chosen fright wig or an over-ambitious set of false teeth are sure to lead to your unmasking. Less can often be more, so avoid

overplaying your hand. Avoid passing yourself off as somebody much older or younger than you actually are, or of a vastly different body shape or even gender.

Work on expressions

Holmes used artificial aids such as make-up to adapt his look (on one occasion he even rubbed his eyes with nightshade to make himself appear seriously ill) but equally important was his ability to adopt seemingly authentic expressions. Thus, in 'The Empty House', we have a bookseller sporting a 'snarl of contempt' so effective that Watson entirely fails to recognise his old friend. Similarly, in 'The Final Problem' he convincingly adopts a protruding lower lip and a habit of mumbling. Here Holmes's grasp of body language proved a useful skill.

Know your accents

Having the ability to take on a new voice is a brilliant way to mislead. Holmes was presumably masterful in Norwegian and in 'His Last Bow' passed himself off as a convincing Irish-American.

Have a back story

Know your alter ego inside out so that if you are challenged, you may maintain it effortlessly. It is difficult to imagine that Holmes could have so effectively masqueraded as Sigerson unless he had a deep knowledge of the Norwegian's life story.

Commit to the part

At times you may be forced to go the extra mile to maintain a deception. One of Sherlock's favourite techniques was to stoop in order to appear older. 'It is no joke when a tall man has to take a foot off his stature for several hours on end,' he was forced to complain. Even more startlingly, in 'The Adventure of Charles Augustus Milverton', Holmes found himself engaged to a housemaid called Agatha, all in the cause of maintaining the illusion of his disguise.

Quiz 16 – Elementary, dear reader ... Part III

A mugger accosts a wizened old riddler in one of Soho's most notorious backstreets.

'Give me your money,' demands the attacker.

The riddler duly takes out his wallet and to the amazement of the thief, counts out thirteen pound notes. 'This is all I have in the world,' he says. 'If you can guess the ages of my three sons from the clues I give you, I'll surrender it without a struggle. If you get it wrong, I'll fight you for it. I might still lose my money as I am not as young as I once was, but I have spirit and I'll make sure you get a good kicking in the process. Are you game?'

The bewildered thief nods.

'Right. If you multiply the ages of my sons together, you get thirty-six. Add them together, and it equals the number of pound notes you've just watched me count. How old are they?'

The thief looks perplexed, numbers spinning chaotically inside his brain. A minute or two later, the riddler says, 'In fairness, I haven't given enough information for you to answer. One more clue. My eldest boy's mathematics tutor is called Professor Gibson. Now that should be all the information you require.'

The thief is as confused as ever. After a few moments he says, 'No, it's no good. I can't possibly figure it out. Explain it to me or I shall lie awake all night wondering about it.'

'With pleasure,' says the riddler, before felling his assailant with a swift kick to the shin and waddling off into the safety of the night.

So what answer should the mugger have given to claim the riddler's money and save himself a nasty bruise?

Breaking the Code

'I am fairly familiar with all forms of secret
writings, and am myself the author of a trifling
monograph upon the subject, in which I analyze
one hundred and sixty separate ciphers.'
'THE ADVENTURE OF THE DANCING MEN'

Cryptography (from the Greek for 'hidden writing') is
the science of code- and cipher-creating, while
cryptanalysis is concerned with breaking them. In
Holmes's world, filled with deceits and intrigues, a
thorough comprehension of cryptanalysis was an
invaluable way to discover useful information.

Some basics to begin with – a code and a cipher are
not the same:

In a code, each word or phrase is replaced by another word, phrase or symbol. Both the message sender and recipient must know what the coded words, phrases and symbols mean either by prior agreement or through use of tools such as code books. A code is a secret language.

In a cipher, each letter is either replaced by an alternative letter, number or symbol (a substitution cipher) or the letters are shuffled about (a transposition cipher). Plaintext is the name given to the information you wish to communicate, while ciphertext is what is actually sent.

Here are a few of history's more famous codes and ciphers:

The Caesar cipher
(also known as the Caesar shift)

This was supposedly devised by Julius Caesar for use by his troops. It involves shifting letters along the alphabet by a set number of positions. If you move the alphabet by one position, for instance, a is signified by b and b is signified by c. So the word cat would be communicated as dbu. Shift two positions and a is signified by c and b is signified by d (with cat becoming ecv). There are a potential twenty-five Caesar shift alphabets.

The transposition code

In its simplest form, this involves writing your message into a grid of suitable size, which is then read from a predetermined start point and in a particular direction. Can you decode the following message?

R	K	W
U	C	Y
O	A	M
H	T	E
E	T	N
N	A	E
O	L	E
N	L	H
I	I	T

Start at the bottom right-hand corner and read each column from bottom to top. The message is 'The enemy will attack in one hour.'

Pig Latin
This technique was probably developed in the early Victorian era. Its basic rules are simple. If a word starts with a consonant (or consonant cluster), move that to the end of the word and add the letters 'ay' after it. If a word begins with a vowel (or a silent consonant), add 'way' to the end. Try deciphering this:

ewarebay ethay angryway anmay inway ethay oldway athay.

The message reads: 'Beware the angry man in the old hat.'

The pigpen cipher

A centuries-old cipher that uses four simple grids containing all the letters of the alphabet:

When writing their message, the sender replaces each letter with the relevant fragment of grid. Hence 'Beware' becomes:

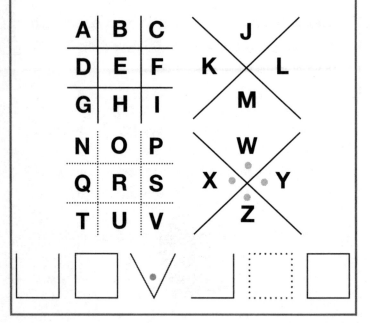

Jargon code

Here a seemingly arbitrary phrase is used in place of a known word or phrase. So, for instance, 'The spider has spun his web from the queen to the Eiffel Tower' might easily be read by a recipient in the know as 'Professor Moriarty (the spider) has taken a train (has spun his web) from Victoria station (the queen) to Paris (the Eiffel Tower)'.

Morse Code

A remarkable code that may be rendered by long and short bursts of sound, flashes of lights, or written dots and dashes. Devised by Samuel Morse in the 1830s, it is still widely used today.

Cryptanalysis works by trying to establish a pattern in coded material. Once a pattern is recognised, breaking a cipher or code becomes achievable. One of the greatest weapons in the arsenal of the cryptanalyst is 'frequency analysis'. This relies on the fact that in almost all languages, certain letters are used more frequently than others. As an example, e is the most common letter in English so there is a reasonable possibility (though not a certainty) that a symbol appearing most often in a ciphertext represents e.

Cryptanalysis is harder today than it has ever been, with new technologies allowing for more complex codes and ciphers. One of the most legendarily difficult to break was the Enigma code employed by German forces during the Second World War. The Enigma machine, a typewriter-like device, relied on a series of rotors that could be set in billions of combinations, allowing for plaintext to be delivered as seemingly impenetrable ciphertext. However, even this machine had weaknesses. A team of brilliant minds housed at Bletchley Park eventually broke the code. They were helped in part by frequency analysis, as they knew certain phrases (such as the names of German generals) recurred often in the encrypted messages. This gave the Allies a huge advantage in the war.

Given the complex challenges of cryptanalysis, it is little surprise that Holmes trained himself to excel at the art. As well as the monograph alluded to in the quote at the beginning of this section, he is witnessed breaking one word puzzle (in 'The Musgrave Ritual'), three codes (in 'The Adventure of the "Gloria Scott"', 'The Adventure of the Red Circle' and *The Valley of Fear*) and the famous stick-figure cipher in 'The Adventure of the Dancing Men'. See how well you get on with breaking the following codes:

Quiz 17 – Say What?

In each case, decipher or decode the devilish encryption!

1. 23,1,20,19,15,14 / 2,18,9,14,7 / 25,15,21,18 / 7,21,14.
2. Tifsmpdl Ipmnft nbef ijt efcvu jo B Tuvez jo Tdbsmfu.

3. Pd Imfeaz ime tue nqef rduqzp.

4. gt obrea kthi scod erequire sjus t abi to flatera lthinkin.

5. ..... / – --- --- -.- / .- / -- .- --. -. .. .. ..-. -.-- .. -.--. / --. .-.. .- ... ... / ..-. .-. --- -- / .... / .--. --- -.-. .-. . - .-.-.-

6.

7. Heavy elephants learn pottery making enthusiastically.

8. A subtle plan is never discovered. Would Henry send his own man to help with the arduous money-bagging starting immediately.

Information Sifting

'It is of the highest importance in the art of
detection to be able to recognise out of a number
of facts which are incidental and which are vital.'
'SILVER BLAZE'

As Holmes amply illustrated, information may be
gleaned from myriad sources. But once a body of
relevant information has been accumulated, the next
trick is to separate the wheat from the chaff: that which
is truly useful and that which ultimately will lead you
down a blind alley. The Great Detective was a master at
streamlining his knowledge to suit his purposes. It is a
lesson well-learned, especially for those of us living at a
time when the prospect of drowning in a sea of data has
never been greater.

There are plenty of real-life examples of
information overload hindering a criminal
investigation. Take the case of Peter Sutcliffe, The
Yorkshire Ripper, who was convicted of killing thirteen
women and attacking seven more in the North of

England in the 1970s and 1980s. The investigation, undertaken at a time when computer technology was still in its infancy, was infamous for paperwork so mountainous that vital clues contained within it were missed. It was even reported that the floor of the main incident room had to be reinforced to deal with the weight of all the documentation. Furthermore, investigating officers wasted time on wild goose chases (such as investigating hoax audio tapes said to have come from the Ripper) while Sutcliffe slipped through their hands several times until his arrest and conviction in 1981.

Not even Holmes was immune to prioritising the wrong leads now and again. In 'The Yellow Face', he comes up with a theory about the case that 'at least covers all the facts. When new facts come to our knowledge which cannot be covered by it, it will be time enough to reconsider it.' Watson, though, calls it 'all surmise' and so it proves when Holmes is found to be far from correct in his assertions. Hindered in this case by the absence of vital information, Holmes failed to sift the data he did have correctly.

Here are a few suggestions as to how to sift your data more efficiently:

Have control over your data
That is to say, you must master it, rather than it you. Gather together all the information you have in as logical a system as you can. Wading through huge piles of information fragments is not conducive to effective sifting.

Keep an eye on the bigger picture
Always keep in mind the big puzzle that you are trying to solve when considering if you have a small piece of it in your hand.

Give yourself time and space to evaluate the information
Spending hours on end staring at data is not the best way to analyse it. Indeed, you might be one of those people whose optimum thinking is done in the shower or while going for a run.

Don't be over-reliant on intuition

It is useful to have a gut-instinct about whether to trust one piece of information more than another. But beware of dismissing information on a whim. And always ask the question: do I have all the pertinent information?

Beware the 'recency' effect

We have a tendency to prioritise the information that we have most recently acquired. Recency and relevance are not inherently linked.

Retain the chaff

Until you have successfully worked through your 'wheat' and solved your conundrum, you may need to revisit the 'chaff' to see if there is anything you have missed.

The job of information sifting is easier if your note-taking powers are up to scratch. The secret to good notes, as any exasperated university lecturer will tell you, is not to take down verbatim accounts. Such an approach ensures that data will slip seamlessly in and immediately out of your brain. The trick is to actively engage with the material you are taking notes on, encode it in a way meaningful to you and reference it to your own knowledge. What does this mean in practice?

> You must grasp the point of the information you are taking notes on.

Cut out any extraneous information as you note-take. For instance, if you are working from a textbook, you might begin by highlighting short passages that best carry the point of the text. Similarly, if you are taking notes while someone is speaking, you should not jot down their verbal ticks or detail long examples given to reinforce a simple point. By being selective in what you note down, you are engaging with the material and have already started the sifting process.

If your initial note-taking process leaves you with rather scruffy notes, re-inscribe them neatly at the earliest opportunity. The longer you leave it, the more notes you are likely to accumulate, and the thought of writing them up neatly will become less appealing.

Use devices to make your notes as easy to review as possible. Most simply, use headings and subheadings. This will add structure to what you write and how you think.

Consider more complex devices too. Will a graph or a diagram make a point most clearly? Colour-coding is another way to make notes visually stimulating. You might write up a main point in blue ink, illustrate with an example in green ink and add some concluding thoughts in red.

One popular way to visually present interconnected ideas or subject matter is the spidergram, also known as the mind map. Spidergrams are a great and simple way to concentrate a lot of ideas in a small space, making review easy and often prompting new trains of thoughts by giving you an overview of the big picture. Here's how you might create one:

At the centre of a blank piece of paper, write your key word or phrase.

Draw lines from this central concept. Each new branch (or spider's leg) connects to a related idea or thought.

Impose some order. Don't let the spidergram get out of control. If there is a clear hierarchy of ideas, number the sections or use a radial hierarchy.

Let your creativity run free. Feel free to use a mixture of upper and lower case printing, different colours, symbols or images. You set the rules.

Here is an example of a spidergram that Holmes might have drawn for 'The Adventure of the Speckled Band':

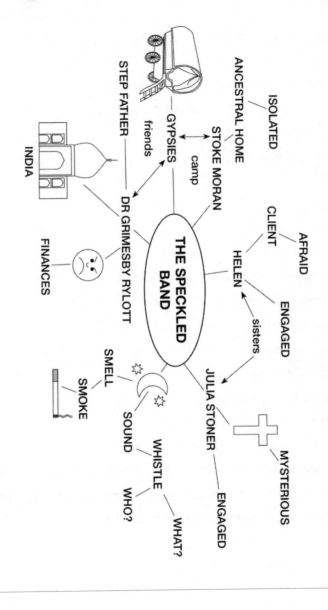

Improving Your Memory

'My mind is like a crowded box-room with
packets of all sorts stowed away therein – so many
that I may well have but a vague perception of
what was there.'
'THE ADVENTURE OF THE LION'S MANE'

Having accumulated the wealth of data required for
your Holmesian-style thinking, it is vital to ensure it
becomes firmly lodged in your memory. Holmes seems
to have had little problem with memory, able to pluck
from the air tiny details of conversation long after they
have occurred or recalling crime reports from years
past. But what is memory? In short, it is the way that
the brain encodes pieces of information so that we may
store them for later retrieval.

The science of memory is continually evolving and
we are still in the early stages of understanding how it
works. However, it is generally accepted that there are
several major classifications of memory:

Sensory memory

This relates to a timescale lasting well under a second from the moment of perception. For instance, you might look at a stream of cars coming down the motorway and process the colour of each car you see but would be unable to recall this data within a few hundred milliseconds of observing it.

Short-term memory

This relates to recall lasting from a few seconds to a minute. On average, a healthy adult can store between four and seven items in this way. Short-term memory allows you to memorise a chunk of a telephone number for quick retrieval a few moments later.

Long-term memory

This type allows us to store huge swathes of information, sometimes created in the earliest years of our life and kept with us to the grave. So while we might use our short-term memory to store a phone number for the local pizza delivery company just until we can get to the phone, our long-term memory allows us to retain the phone number from our childhood home for decades.

There are two main ways to improve memory: through external aids such as an appointments diary or through internal aids, such as certain mental techniques.

External aids are fine for filling certain gaps but there are disadvantages to becoming over-reliant upon them. While there is no problem in using an alarm clock day in and day out to remind us to get up, we might not want to rely on writing too many reminder notes to ourselves simply because it becomes inconvenient. Many studies also suggest that an over-reliance on external aids can make our memories lazier and less able to function without them.

Internal aids are certainly the way forward when it comes to improving our all-important long-term memory. Here are a few techniques you might want to try:

Make it personal

Relate new information to things that are particular to you. This might be anything from people that you know or your favourite sports team to more complex associations incorporating your personal beliefs. You've met a girl whose favourite perfume is Chanel No.5 and you want to remember it so you can buy her a bottle for Christmas. Is the number five your lucky number? Was it your shirt number in the school sports team? Your house number? Make a link.

Use imagery

Need a way to remember someone's name? Just been introduced to Mr Glass? Then imagine Mr Glass as being see-through. Next time the two of you meet, it will be the first thing that pops into your head and you'll have no problem recalling his name. Alas, not everyone will have such an imagery-friendly name, but the only limit to this system is your own imagination.

Say it proud

Not always a convenient technique, but repeating aloud a vital bit of information gives you more chance of remembering it.

Remember just as you are about to forget

This was the conclusion of a nineteenth century German psychologist called Hermann Ebbinghaus. Having spent many years testing his recall of lengthy strings of random nonsense, he discerned that the most efficient memorisation goes on during the earliest attempts. Although less new information is retained in each subsequent review, the memory is reinforced so reviews need only occur at ever more distant moments in time. Thus, you should review new information initially after just a few seconds, then after a few minutes, then after an hour and so on. Eventually, you might only need to re-remember a memory every few years for it to remain intact.

Chunking

A useful method for items like strings of numbers, addresses, etc. Imagine you need to remember a twelve-digit bank card number: 196674722199. It will be a lot easier to fix it in your memory if you divide it up into sections: 1966 7472 2199. And if you can attach some meaning to each chunk, it becomes easier still. For instance, you might wish to remember it in these chunks: 1966 (the year England won the World Cup) 747 (a jumbo jet) 221 (Sherlock's number on Baker Street) 99 (red balloons).

Mnemonics

This is a nice verbal trick to lodge a clump of information in your mind. Many of the most effective mnemonics are nothing more than simple acronyms. Thus, the eminently memorable line 'Richard of York gave battle in vain' reminds us of the colours of the rainbow (red, orange, yellow, green, blue, indigo, violet) while 'Naughty elephants squirting water' reminds us of the order of the compass points (north, east, south, west).

Implementation intentions

If you need to remember to do something on a regular basis, then this might work for you. It is a system of self-regulation so that you might tell yourself, 'I must take my pills with my cup of tea just before bedtime'.

Brain-training games

Sudoku and crosswords are considered an excellent way to preserve memory faculty and can help fend off conditions such as Alzheimer's Disease.

Put your memories in their place

This is a technique employed by some of the world's leading exponents of memory feats, so let's look at it in a little more detail after a quick break for a quiz ...

Quiz 18 – Elementary, dear reader ... Part IV

Archie is the getaway driver for a gang of robbers who plan to rob a local post office. They enter the shop at quarter to six in the evening and hold up the staff as they are cashing up for the day. The robbers have told Archie to have the motor running and ready to go at six o'clock precisely.

Sure enough, from his driver's seat, Archie watches the gang enter the post office at a quarter to six. Ten minutes later, he looks at the clock on the dashboard and sees that it is five to six. A minute later it says, as expected, four minutes to six. But when he looks again two minutes later, it still says four minutes to six. 'The time sure drags when you're tense,' he thinks to himself. A minute later he looks at the clock again. Now it says the time is five to six. Utterly bewildered, he starts to panic. Is time really going backwards? Is he losing his mind? A minute later, he looks once more at the clock, realises he is actually quite sane and hurriedly powers up the engine as the gang emerge from the post office, swag-bags in hand. What was happening to time?

Taking a Walk Down Memory Lane

'A man should keep his little brain attic stocked
with all the furniture that he is likely to use.'
'THE FIVE ORANGE PIPS'

This memory method relies on your intimate
knowledge of a place and is particularly useful for
memorising a lot of connected information, such as a
list. Once you have mastered it, you should be able to
recall a list of items far longer than the traditional seven
or so.

This technique goes under a number of different
names. Some know it as the Memory Palace, others as
the Method of Loci or the Roman Room Technique,
to name but a few. Underlying the system is the
selection of a place that you know really well such as

your current home, or one from your childhood, or perhaps the local high street or the office (especially if you're a workaholic). You could even focus on a single room if it has lots of elements in it that you are familiar with.

Let's say you've opted for your childhood home. You then need to fix firmly in your mind a route through the house. Start with your key in the front door. Open the door and step into the hallway. Plot a path taking in all the different rooms, upstairs and downstairs. Once you have the route established, you can use it again and again, every time there is a new list of information you want to memorise.

If there are more things to remember than there are rooms in the house, consider developing the system so that as you walk your route, you take in several features in each room. For instance, rather than associating only one thing with the kitchen, you could picture your fridge, the kitchen table, the toaster and the sink. That's space for four new things.

Each of the familiar elements on your route is known as a 'memory peg'. The job now is to hang each item you wish to remember on a different peg. Let's say you are off to the shops but you can't find a pen so you need to carry your shopping list in your head. The first item is a bottle of milk, which we'll place on the front door step. The next is a newspaper, which we'll conveniently slot into the letter box. Next is half a dozen eggs. These we place on the living room mantelpiece to use in place of vases. Meanwhile, the shirt you want to buy is hanging in the front room window where the curtains normally are. It doesn't matter how weird things get in your memory palace. In fact, the stranger things are, the easier they are to remember.

The more you use this technique, the more elements you will be able to remember. Some experts claim to be able to recall hundreds of things in this manner.

But that's enough of the theory. See how you get on with these challenges, perhaps using one or more of the techniques above. The first of the following two exercises will test your short-term memory, while the latter will give a work-out to your long-term memory.

Quiz 19 – Total Recall

Look at the items collected from a murder scene for one minute. When the minute is up, turn over the page and attempt to list all the pieces of evidence on a separate sheet of paper.

Quiz 20 – Remembering that Crime Doesn't Pay

Have a look at the following list of criminals and their convictions. Once you have read and absorbed the information, turn the page and read on. Wait for ten minutes, then try to write down the details of each of the convictions. Wait a further half an hour and repeat. Do it again in a few hours. How has your memory coped?

1. One-legged Mary got ten years for battering her husband with her wooden crutch.
2. Skinny Jim was fined two pounds and ten shillings for stealing a loaf of bread.
3. Dead-eye Pete was hanged for shooting dead a rival poker player.
4. Burlington Bertie got three years for defrauding a jeweller.
5. Nervous Ned was shot at dawn for deserting from the army.
6. Buxom Bella: three months for soliciting.
7. Angry Alexander was thrown into the clink for two nights for being drunk and disorderly.

Reaching Conclusions

> 'It is an old maxim of mine that when you have
> excluded the impossible, whatever remains,
> however improbable, must be the truth.'
> 'THE ADVENTURE OF THE BERYL CORONET'

Holmes's gift (and occasional curse) was his unearthly ability to alight upon the truth where others had failed to do so. To conclude your crash course in thinking like the Great Detective, let's take a look at the modus operandi he used to reach the right answer so often:

Be in the right frame of mind
Seeking the truth is an exercise best done when rested and relaxed. Fuel yourself too. A team of researchers in 2010 found that making judgements is best achieved when your blood sugar levels are at their optimum level.

Gather your raw information
As we have seen, Holmes gathered data from a huge range of sources - the crime scene, eye-witnesses, personal experience, reference materials etc.

Evaluate the data
Set aside that which seems flawed or not useful.

Be a reader of human nature
In *The Sign of Four,* Holmes quoted the historian and philosopher, Winwood Reade, on the subject:

He remarks that, while the individual man is an insoluble puzzle, in the aggregate he becomes a mathematical certainty. You can, for example, never foretell what any one man will do, but you can say with precision what an average number will be up to. Individuals vary, but percentages remain constant. So says the statistician.

Search for the anomaly
The out-of-place detail can be the thread that unravels an enigma. As Holmes said, 'what is out of the common is usually a guide rather than a hindrance.'

Think the unthinkable

As Holmes proclaimed in *The Valley of Fear,* 'how often is imagination the mother of truth?'

Formulate your hypotheses

Evaluate the likelihood of each hypothesis against the known facts. When Holmes was accused of straying into guesswork in *The Hound of the Baskervilles,* he responded: 'Say, rather, into the region where we balance probabilities and choose the most likely. It is the scientific use of the imagination, but we have always some material basis on which to start our speculation.'

Don't mistake correlation for causation

As an example, we live in an age when the ice caps are melting and obesity is increasing, but that does not mean one causes the other or that they are linked in any way beyond coincidence.

Be rigorous

Do not become fixated on a single particular theory. Entertain all the possibilities.

Exclude the impossible ...

Perhaps Holmes's guiding maxim — a hypothesis that does not fit the facts must be dismissed. Eventually you will be left with the only theory which complies with all the facts. No matter how unlikely it seems, this must be the truth.

Now, to paraphrase the Great Detective, you now know his methods. Use them!

Answers to Quizzes

Answers to Quiz 1 – Letter Scramble

Page 27 – DR WATSON
           SHERLOCK HOLMES

Page 28 – MAGNIFYING GLASS
           SCOTLAND YARD

Answers to Quiz 2 – Number Sequences

1. 64 (the number doubles each time).
2. 729 (the number multiplies by three each time).
3. 49 (these are the first seven square numbers).
4. 17 (these are the first seven prime numbers).
5. 22, 18 (figures in the even numbered positions increase in steps of two, while figures in odd numbered positions reduce by three).
6. 89 (this is the Fibonacci series in which each figure is the sum of the previous two).
7. 8 (each figure is the product of all the digits in the previous figure).

Answers to Quiz 3 – Word Ladders

i)
Cat
Cot
Hot
Hod
Hid
Kid

ii)
Game
Lame
Lome
Lose
Lost
Loot
Foot

Answers to Quiz 4 – Word Wheel

Name: DRWATSON

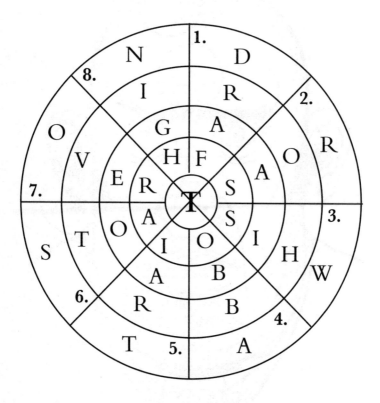

Answers to Quiz 5 – Not a Pretty Picture

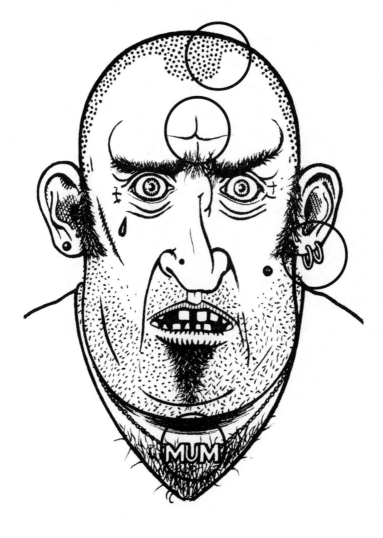

Answers to Quiz 6 – Speed Reading

1. Four pounds per week.
2. The *Encyclopedia Britannica*.
3. From ten until two.
4. Ink, pens and blotting paper.
5. On Thursday and Friday evening.

Answers to Quiz 7 – Lost for Words

1. out (breakout and outstanding).
2. moon (honeymoon and moonbeam).
3. house (greenhouse and housecoat).
4. book (notebook and bookkeeper).
5. man (policeman and manhole).
6. wall (stonewall and wallpaper).
7. play (screenplay and playtime).

Answers to Quiz 8 – Dingbats

1. 'The Adventure of the Speckled Band'
2. 'A Scandal in Bohemia'
3. 'Silver Blaze'
4. 'The Crooked Man'
5. 'The Adventure of the Dancing Men'
6. 'The Adventure of the Red Circle' (communism)
7. 'The Adventure of the Six Napoleons'
8. 'The Adventure of the Missing Three-Quarter'
9. 'The Adventure of the Empty House'
10. 'The Adventure of the Copper Beeches'

Answers to Quiz 9 – What Next?

1. 1 Samuel and 2 Samuel. The sequence is the first ten books of the Old Testament.

2. S and S. For Saturday and Sunday. The sequence is the initials of the days of the week.

3. 30 and 31. The sequence shows the number of days in each month from January to December.

4. U and N. For Uranus and Neptune. The sequence is the initial letters of the planets in the solar system by distance from the sun: Mercury, Venus, Earth, Mars, Jupiter, Saturn, Uranus and Neptune.

5. K and L. The sequence is the letters from left to right on the second row of a QWERTY keyboard.

6. London and Rio de Janeiro. The sequence is the last ten host cities of the Summer Olympic Games up to 2016.

7. 1936 and 1952. The sequence is the years in which a new monarch has come to the English throne since the restoration of the monarchy with the crowning of Charles II.

8. Serbia and South Sudan. A real teaser! The sequence is of the world's eight newest countries as recognised by the United Nations.

Answers to Quiz 10 – What on Earth?

1. The customer had hiccups. This was why he asked for a glass of water. The barman cured him by giving him a shock.
2. Louise.
3. Tom put down a pound coin, while Dick paid with five twenty pence pieces.
4. Never mind whether its legal, it's impossible. If the woman has a widower, she must be dead!
5. They shouldn't be buried. The survivors are alive.

6. Take a piece of fruit from the box marked 'Oranges & Lemons' (which we know is incorrectly labelled). Say you pick out an orange, then you know that box should be labelled 'Oranges'. The box labelled 'Lemons' must thus be relabelled 'Oranges & Lemons' and the box originally marked 'Oranges' needs the 'Lemons' label.

7. The van.

Answers to Quiz 11 – Most Irregular

Irregular	Distinguishing feature	Station
Wiggins	Wears a waistcoat	Farringdon Street
Smiffy	Has red hair	King's Cross
Jimmy	Wears a crumpled hat	Portland Road
Tommy	Trousers rolled up at the knee	Gower Street
Johnny	Has a scar on his chin	Baker Street

Answers to Quiz 12 – CSI Baker Street

1. He used a block of ice to stand on to kill himself.

2. He was jumping out of an aeroplane but his parachute failed to open.

3. Benny and some friends had hired a hot air balloon to inspect the scene of Kenny's death. The balloon got into problems and started to lose height. The people on board threw any extraneous items overboard, including their clothes, in the hope of halting their plummet but to no avail. In the end they drew straws to see who would sacrifice themselves to save the others by leaping out and reducing the weight still further. Benny picked the short straw.

4. Dave was sucked out of the sea into the water tank of a fire service aeroplane, which was collecting water to dowse the forest fire.

5. Bobby was the name of the snowman the boy had made the day before but which has melted overnight.

6. The car is a convertible. The roof is down. The murderer simply shot him from the pavement and dropped the weapon into the back of the car before fleeing.

Answers to Quiz 13 – Holmes Trivia

1. John (though on one occasion in the stories he is referred to as James).
2. The Vernets.
3. Stamford.
4. Opera singer and adventuress.
5. Mary Morstan.
6. Professor Moriarty.
7. University of London.
8. Mycroft.
9. The Diogenes Club.
10. The Reichenbach Falls.
11. 221B Baker Street.
12. Consulting detective.
13. The Sussex Downs.
14. In the toe of a Persian slipper.
15. A drunken unemployed groom or a clergyman.
16. Devon.
17. Wiggins.

18. The 'Gloria Scott'.

19. They were narrated by Sherlock Holmes himself, rather than Dr Watson.

20. In a tin dispatch box in the vaults of the bank of Cox & Co. in Charing Cross.

Answer to Quiz 14 – Elementary, dear reader … Part I

At number eighty-one. For the police to be sure they had the right property, the answers they received from the informant must have offered up only one possible number. The only way this is possible is if the informant answered no to the first question and yes to the other two.

Answer to Quiz 15 – Elementary, dear reader ... Part II

Billy Goldfingers. If it was Tom, Billy and Joe would both be telling the truth. If it was Jack, then each of the other three is being honest. And if it was Joe, then neither Jack nor Billy is telling lies. But if it's Billy, then only Joe is not fibbing.

Answer to Quiz 16 – Elementary, dear reader ... Part III

The riddler's sons are aged two, two and nine. The mugger saw the riddler count out thirteen pounds (unlucky for the assailant). He had got as far as working out the eight possible combinations of three numbers that when multiplied together equal thirty-six.

1, 1 and 36
1, 2 and 18
1, 3 and 12

1, 4 and 9

1, 6 and 6

2, 2 and 9

2, 3 and 6

3, 3 and 4

However, two of these combinations add up to thirteen (1, 6 and 6, as well as 2, 2 and 9), leaving the mugger confused as to which ages the children are. But he should have listened carefully to the riddler, who spoke of his 'eldest' son. This confirms that his boys must be aged two, two and nine.

Answers to Quiz 17 – Say What?

1. Watson bring your gun. (A simple code based on numbers in place of letters, with a = 1, b = 2 and so on).

2. Sherlock Holmes made his debut in *A Study in Scarlet*. (A Caesar cipher, with the alphabet shifted along by one letter.)

3. Dr Watson was his best friend. (A more complicated Caesar cipher, with the alphabet shifted twelve places so that 'M' represents 'A'.)

4. To break this code requires just a bit of lateral thinking. In this code, the last letter of each word becomes the first letter of the proceeding word. The last letter of the whole sentence moves to the start.

5. He took a magnifying glass from his pocket. (This is Morse code.)

6. The hansom cab sped down Baker Street. (This is semaphore.)

7. Help me. (The key to this code is to read the first letter of each word.)

8. Plan discovered. Send man with money immediately. (The plaintext is revealed by reading every third word, much like the code Holmes broke in 'The Advenure of "Gloria Scott"'.)

Answer to Quiz 18 – Elementary, dear reader …
Part IV

The clock on the dashboard was digital, and the top-right vertical stroke of the last digit was not working. Therefore, when Archie looked at the clock at five to six, it read:

17:55

A minute later:

17:56

Two minutes later:

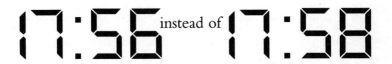

A minute later:

And at six o'clock:

18:06

Answers to Quiz 19 – Total Recall

A penknife.

A pill bottle.

Some coins.

A bank card.

A cinema ticket.

A set of keys.

A teacup.

A pair of glasses.

A mobile phone.

A pen.

An envelope.